Irving Finkel, the author, works in the British Museum, where he reads cuneiform inscriptions from ancient Mesopotamia. His previous works for children include *The Lewis Chessmen and What Happened to Them* and *Gilgamesh the Hero*. He lives in London and has five children.

Emily Donegan, the illustrator, won the BBC Blue Peter Competition to design a poster for the 250th anniversary of the British Museum in June 2003. She lives in Bangor, Northern Ireland, where she goes to school. This is Emily's first book.

The author is happy to admit it that he is 40 years older than the artist, who produced the first illustrations for this story when she was 12 years old.

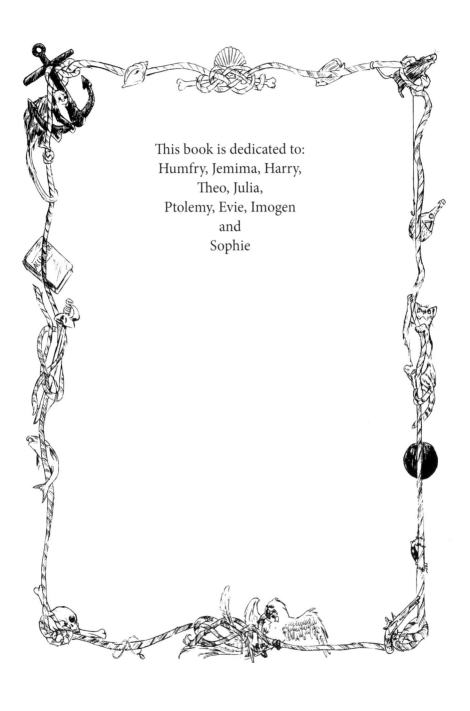

This book is dedicated to:
Humfry, Jemima, Harry,
Theo, Julia,
Ptolemy, Evie, Imogen
and
Sophie

Alfred
and the Pirates

Irving Finkel

Illustrated by
Emily Donegan

PARROT
BOOKS

First published 2006 by Parrot Books (UK)

Parrot Books (UK) is an imprint of Archetype Publications Ltd.
6 Fitzroy Square
London W1T 5HJ

www.archetype.co.uk

Tel: 44(207) 380 0800
Fax: 44(207) 380 0500

© Text Irving Finkel 2006
© Illustrations Emily Donegan 2006

Cover artwork, Emily Donegan

ISBN 1-904982-10-7

British Library Cataloguing in Publication Data
A catalogue record for this book is available from the British Library.

Printed and bound by Gutenberg Press Limited, Malta

begins, however, Alfred Appletree had just reached the age of thirteen and three-quarters. What Josephine Jellicoe called his 'pirate days' were long over, and anyone who had known him would have said the same.

Perhaps he would tell Josephine about the dream. She was always talking about things like dreams and the future. Alfred had been friends with her since primary school and now at the new school they happened to be desk partners. Most of the boys in Alfred's class who had sisters made a great show of thinking that all girls were daft, if not worse. Alfred had neither brothers nor sisters, but he certainly liked Josephine, and she liked him. Josephine was a good listener when she stopped talking.

The effects of this dream were still all over him. He still felt that he was about to fall one hundred feet down through the holes in a giant spider's web of rigging. And there was a vague feeling that someone was after him. He couldn't shake it off and he shivered on the mat, despite the warmth of the bathroom.

Pirates.

What business had they butting in like that, invading his life and his mind like a load of whirling dervishes?

Chapter Three

At breakfast, he sat staring at the back of the cereal box with his spoon in the air, suddenly hearing the cry of gulls in his ears.

'Have you got everything ready for school?' asked his mother again. 'It's a new term, a new year. And an important one.'

Alfred sighed. His father put down his newspaper and tapped him on the shoulder.

'Nothing's been tampered with, you know, son. We had the new food-taster in just this morning, and everything on the table is guaranteed.'

Alfred dropped his spoon, groaned heavily, and fell off his chair onto the floor.

'Good *gracious* Alfie,' cried his mother at the toaster, knocking over her own chair. 'Whatever's the matter?'

'We've … been … betrayed.'

He twitched violently then lay on his back with his legs in the air, never to move again. His father finished his own mouthful, lowered his spoon, and stood up weakly.

'Call the Guard! Treachery! Save the dynasty!'

He groaned pitifully and clutching his stomach with both hands, staggered out in the hall to collect his briefcase.

'This place gets more like a kindergarten every day,' said Mrs Appletree, scraping carbon off her toast. 'I don't know which of you is worse.'

'Just wait till you feel the effects,' said her husband, from the hall, tying his shoelace, 'you'll see.'

He came back in and kissed his wife, gave his son a salute and left for work. Alfred got back up at the table and drank his tea. There were no symptoms to be observed in his mother.

'Incidentally, Alfred, I have a class here this morning, don't forget. Before you depart, perhaps you could clear out that stuff from the front room so I can hoover before they arrive? I'd be very grateful. You've still got enough time.'

'They' were a group of ladies of mixed ages and shapes who came looking for vigour and vim with the help of Mrs Appletree and various aerobic processes. Alfred and his father had been known to conduct their own exercises in the hall to accompany her instructions, without her knowing, although once she had caught them at it.

Alfred went reluctantly down the steps into the street, wearing his school rucksack, a pirate on the way to the classroom.

He had straight black hair which always looked too long at the back because his neck was skinny. Alfred was by inclination quite a solitary boy, although he didn't mind dealing with other people when he had to. His grandmother thought he was much too thin, and so did Mrs Appletree, but his father said that Alfred had a high metabolic rate like himself at the same age and not to fuss. Mr Appletree was quite round and comfortable now, and very slightly shorter than Mrs Appletree.

Alfred's house was quite near Josephine's, but there was no sign of her. She *would* be especially early on the first day of term. Josephine had untidy brown hair, delicate hands and rarely sat still for long. Probably a high metabolic rate too, Alfred thought. He had a private name for her, 'Mabe', which had come about because his father, a Napoleon fan, had the irritating habit of saying 'Not tonight Josephine' whenever her name was mentioned, which eventually turned into 'Maybe-Tomorrow', and then 'Mabe'.

He wandered reluctantly through the familiar gates into the yard. Everyone seemed to be there, the complete range of inmates.

Josephine, surrounded by her usual cronies, stuck out her tongue at him. She was very brown, fresh back from the Algarve or somewhere. He pulled on both his ears and rolled his eyes in return.

Migrating between classrooms under an unfamiliar timetable, Alfred got all the news. Someone had a broken leg, someone had left. No-one was dead. The pupils slipped back into their normal groups as if there had been no interruption. It all seemed to be so noisy. Banging and shouting and running about, and already talk of 'good performance' and the threat of examinations.

The morning wore on. It was now French conversation, of all things, and everybody was rusty – except those who had been to France and wanted to show off. Alfred was experimenting in his mind, trying to imagine himself back on the ship, putting out feelers, and didn't notice when he was spoken to. He had a curious desire to 'tune in' on them. There was nothing there, however.

'… Let us turn to our *cher* Alfred, who will certainly know the *réponse* …?'

Josephine kicked him, more painfully than was perhaps absolutely necessary.

'Perhaps, *en effet*, he doesn't,' remarked Miss Chappel, the French teacher. 'How *disappointing*. Perhaps this inattention in a person of your age implies that it is time for lunch, or something?'

Just as she glanced at her watch the bell rang, signifying liberty.

'Lucky stiff,' said Josephine.

'Bruised stiff, you mean,' said Alfred, rubbing his leg. There, in the bright light of the classroom, it didn't seem worth telling her about his dream after all.

She handed Alfred a sheet of paper with several lines of neat print. He read through the titles with a feeling of excitement mixed with despair.

'Do you happen to read French and German?' asked the librarian politely. 'If so, there are some useful-sounding recent publications in those languages – and in Dutch too, it seems.'

'Er …' said Alfred, and stopped. It had never occurred to him that the languages they had to learn at school could ever be put to practical use.

'I have a suggestion,' said the librarian decisively. 'You are evidently a serious historian, so we must find a way around your difficulty. I have a good friend who is the history librarian out at the university. Do you know where the university is, by any chance?'

Alfred did; he had cycled there several times with Josephine. It was some miles out of town.

'I shall write a letter for you to take to the university. Find the library, and go to the main desk at the entrance. Tell the man behind the desk that you would like to speak to Dr Hugo Cholmondley personally. Once you have handed him the letter I think that will do the trick.'

The librarian motioned to him to wait and sat down at her desk. She inserted a sheet of notepaper in an old black typewriter and with great rapidity produced a letter, folded it and tucked it into an envelope. She wrote on the envelope by hand.

'Now, if that line of attack doesn't succeed come straight back here and we'll try again.'

Alfred grinned at her in appreciation and shook her hand through the little window at the enquiry desk.

'Do you think he will be there on a Saturday?' he asked, turning back on an afterthought.

'Probably yes. I believe he's writing a book himself at the moment. Wait a minute. I'll telephone and see, without divulging why I want to know.'

She dialled without looking up the number, spoke into the

receiver for a moment, and gave Alfred the thumbs-up sign. Alfred waved and left the library, holding the envelope safely under his jacket.

These were not books to be read through in five minutes. One was really huge. Alfred had never even seen such a book before. He opened it at random. 'Appendix III: Statistical Analysis' he read. He felt his heart sink.

'I think what we'll do,' said the librarian encouragingly, 'is to install you in an A-for-Alfred seat in the library and let you have a good look at these books, so you can decide whether or not they will be useful. I have to get on with some work myself now. When you are ready, come back here and we shall decide on a strategy.'

Alfred followed him back into the reading room, where they soon found an empty seat in row A. In fact it was seat A 71.

'You have paper, pencil and the like?'

'Oh gosh, I never even thought of that.'

'First requirement for the historian. Don't you worry – I'm sure we can dig something up.'

Chapter Seven

Dr Cholmondley yawned voluminously and looked up from his untidy papers. It was growing dark, he realised, and he was peckish. It was then that he remembered his new recruit and thought that he ought perhaps to take a look at Alfred. It was 6.20pm by his watch and many of the seats in the reading room were now empty.

He found Alfred slumped over the pile of books, sound asleep. Dr Cholmondley registered a sharp sense of disappointment. He had believed that Alfred's interest was genuine and had been gratified to encounter such a grown-up attitude in a boy of Alfred's age. Then he noticed that there were several pages of writing on the desk, the undoubted fruit of hard labour. He reached out to touch the boy on the shoulder. Alfred was very deeply asleep and sweating violently. At the touch he cried out and awoke with a shudder. He looked up at the kindly librarian as at a total stranger, horror and shock still in his eyes.

Dr Cholmondley was not to know, but Alfred had been a thousand leagues and more away. The pirates had leaped off the printed page to call him back, and the journey had truly been a nightmare …

… They were in a longboat, six of them, pulling away from an island. A man was standing on the sand, screaming hysterically, tearing at his straggling hair, shrieking through his tears. Again, the sound travelled across the water with shocking clarity: the noise seemed to be almost on top of them. The oars dipped quietly and steadily as the longboat pulled further and further away from the beach. The voice behind them swelled higher, tinged with madness and terror. It held to a peak of dribbling frenzy and then a shot exploded, cutting off the sound instantly. The rowers paused and looked at one another.

The maroon lay crumpled on the smooth silver sand by his sea chest and half-barrel of supplies. They had left him a gun and ammunition, of course. Tradition demanded it.

'He's topped himself!' said the boatswain.

'Marooned for *five minutes*? What a joke! He'll go down in the record books as the world's biggest weed.'

'We'll be going back for his stores, then,' said the boatswain.

Alfred leaned on the rudder to start turning the boat.

'Mind the brains when you land, bo'sun. On your boots.'

'Brains? I don't think he had that many in the first place ...'

'What had he done?' asked Alfred, concentrating.

'He was a cheap thief. Nicked bits of gold from the hands when they were asleep.'

The boat landed on the shingle, skilfully navigated right up to the body. The head was almost completely gone. Flies had already arrived, too. Alfred tried not to look.

'I was right, Bob,' said the boatswain, tugging at the squat barrel. 'His head was pretty empty ...'

'How did you get here this afternoon, Alfred?' asked Dr Cholmondley gently.

'By bike. It's outside. By the railing.'

'Come on, I'll give you a lift. I'm off now myself.'

In silence, the librarian collected Alfred's pirate books and his notes, and they went back to his room. Alfred walked like a ghost: he was clearly shaken. Dr Cholmondley was a man with children of his own, and knew much better than to question Alfred directly. He waited until the bicycle was stowed in the boot and they had turned the corner out of the campus onto the main road before casually talking of other things, only later asking him, quietly, what had got him interested all of a sudden in the history of pirates.

Alfred told him briefly about the history topic for school and how he wanted to do a really good piece of work.

'And what angle do you think you will take in your essay?'

Faced with this question head on, Alfred suddenly knew what he wanted to do.

'I think I want to describe the difference between pirates in stories that everybody knows, and pirates as they really are' ... he faltered ... 'I mean were.'

'I see,' said Dr Cholmondley, 'that sounds like good historical procedure to me, trying to establish the truth about something in the past. I often wish I could do that myself,' he added, changing gear awkwardly and slowing down at the lights.

Chapter Ten

His parents stood together later that evening, watching their son lying in distress on top of his sheets.

'He'll be OK,' said Mr Appletree, stoutly. 'I think he looks a bit better already.'

Mrs Appletree said nothing. Her apprehension had by no means gone away. Alfred was still far too hot, twisting restlessly and sometimes muttering to himself …

He was, at that moment, right back on the ship. This time he found himself on deck. It was apparently the middle of the day in the middle of a tropical sea. He felt the sweat run on his forehead and temples; the sun beating off the whitened boards made his eyes hurt and his head ache.

There was one sailor nearby on deck. He was a dark, lithe man with a tarred pigtail down his back. He seemed to be quite unaware of Alfred, looking carefully out to sea, concentrating. The ship was rolling slowly and rhythmically, but the pirate stood as if part of the deck himself. His leg muscles moved in unison with the ship as if he had never set foot on dry land.

He wore one earring of gleaming brass – rather like half the boys in Alfred's class – but with that any resemblance to an English schoolboy ended. The sailor, even from behind, looked like a pirate. He was full of lurking energy, swift, decisive movement and unmistakable menace. He must be, thought Alfred, a completely unsentimental killer. The pirate was armed with one straight, cruel knife tucked through his belt. He wore a rough, white open shirt and heavy, dark blue trousers that left most of the lower leg bare. Alfred's mother, in a summer garden, would call them 'cut-offs'.

Somehow the pirate, in these clothes, managed to look almost elegant. His bare feet, with the toes slightly splayed on the planks, looked tougher than boots would ever be. His head was bound in a bright, tightly knotted scarf that only emphasised the hard outline of his skull. He was burnt dark by the sun, and slender. Alfred thought he had never in his life seen anyone so dangerous-looking.

He made a slight, unintentional noise with his foot and the pirate half-turned swiftly, revealing for the first time that he was fishing with a simple line in one hand.

'Oh, there you are, you wretch. I've had to whistle for you twice. Next time, it had better be just once, or I'll split you up the middle and feed you to the fishes. Take this line, and don't lose it. I've got to go below.'

He handed the fishing line to Alfred in a sudden movement and turned on his heel. With a spasm of fear Alfred saw that his face was savagely scarred right across, probably by a blow from a cutlass. He seemed to have only one functional eye, although he wore no conventional eye-patch. Despite the horrid wound he was striking to look at. As he passed by, Alfred noticed with a shock that he was perfumed.

He held the line fearfully. What on earth would he do if something bit at the other end? He was absolutely no fisherman himself, and had only once in his life actually been fishing. That was with Adam from school and Adam's father. His own father always said that fishing was only right if you ate your catch, but on that occasion none of them had caught anything but a couple of measly sticklebacks.

Alfred looked round nervously, but there was no-one else there. He held onto the line tightly, twisting it round his palms and hoping that nothing would happen when he was in charge – although he wasn't entirely sure how much he really wanted the pirate to come back at all. Suddenly there was a violent tug on the line. He held tight defiantly with both hands in self-defence. The pull on the other end quickly grew very much stronger. Alfred struggled to master it, but the line was so tightly bound round his hands that the monstrous fish on the other end began to pull him across the deck instead. Alfred resisted with all his strength, but was unable to save himself. He slid with increasing momentum towards the ship's rail, bracing himself for the worst, when there was a swift, bright flash in the sunlight and he was freed. He crashed into a stanchion and fell over, banging his head. The pirate had reached out and sliced through the taut line with his knife. He had been standing watching Alfred's struggle and decided at the last minute to intervene.

'Good try,' said the pirate, replacing the knife in his belt, 'but with a fish like that you have to stand correctly to take the weight.'

Alfred was unable to move or speak.

'It was probably a big specimen, maybe a swordfish,' said the pirate. 'They like that bait especially.'

'What was it?' said Alfred, eventually.

He had unclenched his hands. They were badly cut by the line and bleeding.

'The bait?' said the pirate, casually. 'Oh, my favourite. *Cabin-boy intestines …*'

Chapter Eleven

Alfred awoke with a jolt, his eyes wide. Mrs Appletree was there, seated by his pillow. She placed another flannel on his forehead and spoke to him soothingly, in a way that she had last done when her son was about four years old. He lay back, exhaustedly, his limbs burning …

The next thing he knew was that he was out of the sun, below decks somewhere. The pirate had carried him below to rub salt into his palms.

'Always do this. After a fight, after a flogging. Nothing wrong with pain if it is doing you good. Shows you're still alive. Different from bullet holes or gangrene, you'll agree?'

Alfred could hardly respond for agony, but he looked around him at the other pirates in the strange, dark-beamed room. There were many hammocks strung around and five or six members of the crew that he could see, obviously off-duty. They were crouched over a low table playing a dice game of some sort.

None of them seemed to find his presence aboard ship strange at all. It was almost as if he had stepped into a play to replace an understudy who had just been waiting for his return. The light was poor and he couldn't see much. He felt very hot and ill. There was a sea-lantern hooked on a beam above his head. It swayed rhythmically and squeaked in time to the movement. Alfred lay and watched it, falling into a restless, tortured sleep that seemed to go on interminably.

He lay in the hammock in swirling delirium. The perfumed sailor came and watched him thrashing about from time to time, simply pouring sea water over him when the fever was at its worst. Sometimes it seemed to Alfred that there were other figures there, separate from the pirate – even people from his childhood – and he dreamed too that a boy with red hair, frightened and persecuted, also came to watch by his hammock.

In time his fever began to diminish, and the morning finally came when he awoke feeling weakened, but more or less himself. He lay on his back in the now-familiar bedding, staring up at the ceiling. He sensed that someone was still watching him and sat up abruptly. His head swam and he felt utterly feeble, but he saw that there was a boy there by the great beam to which the hammock had been roped. He was extremely skinny, with red hair, and looked unaccountably familiar. Then Alfred remembered – he was the boy from the victim ship who had waved from the crow's nest, just before the attack. When *was* that?

'It's you, isn't it? What happened to your ship, your crew?'

'The crew were all murdered and the ship was burned,' said the boy hoarsely. 'I'm the only survivor. They kept me alive – I don't know why. There was blood absolutely everywhere. I … the smell …' He swallowed. 'I was press-ganged onto that ship by a trick. I'm not a sea boy really. I can read and write, although nobody here knows it. I was in London for one day to visit my aunt at Greenwich and woke up next morning in the navy. But I was happy on that ship in the end. They taught me masses. I was the lookout and the only sailor small enough to get in and explore lots of places. Now she's burned and at the bottom, and all my mates gone, savaged to pieces. Do you know, they even …' he stopped.

Alfred sat bolt upright.

'How long have you been on this ship among the pirates?'

'I'm not sure. Two weeks? Something like that.'

But it can't have been *two weeks* since he had first seen the boy? Could it?

'But now you're here they'll kill me for sure. They won't want to feed two boys. They'll chop me up for the octopuses.'

'No they won't,' said Alfred. He felt sure of himself, for some reason. 'How many pirates are there on the ship?' he asked.

'Maybe twenty? If you count the captain, and me and you,' said the boy. 'If I'm a pirate, too. Am I a pirate, do you think?'

'Not unless you want to be.'

They fell silent for a while. The boy shivered.

'They've got a wooden deck plank here,' said the boy in an undertone, 'it's the captain's favourite trick, I heard. They kept some of the sailors from my ship alive after it went down. For a day or two. No food or drink. They were tied up down here until the captain was ready. He is a devil, that captain. Have you seen him yet? He's small, like a weasel, incredibly savage in battle, and he has all the power in this ship. He's the cruellest man in the world. None of his sailors seem to be afraid of him, I can't understand it. They just follow him in everything. Whatever he tells them is their law. You should have seen them all. The blood … I'll never forget it as long as I live. *If* I live.' He stopped.

'Tell me about the plank,' said Alfred slowly. He could feel himself growing stronger as the boy talked.

'They kept them down here, all tied together. No food or water at all. One of the pirates pretended to be a priest one evening and offered to hear their sins, while the other pirates hid and listened. Then, when one of the sailors actually started to confess, they all burst out of their hiding places and mocked and jeered at them. They told them a hundred times that they were going to die horribly, and nothing in the world could save them. I heard everything. One of the sailors gave me something in secret to return to his family if ever I escape. I've got it safe.'

'Go on,' encouraged Alfred, softly.

'Well, the end came on the third day. They were all carried upstairs still tied up in their knots and dumped like potatoes in one of the boats on deck. Two pirates stood guard with bare swords, sneering at them, prodding them and cutting them a bit. Then two more pirates came up from below carrying the deck plank. It's back over there somewhere now.'

He pointed into the darkness.

'It has special holes and things at one end so that it can be lashed firm onto something on the upper deck. It then rests on the hand-rail and juts out over the sea. Quite a long way. It's quite narrow and springy. One of the sailors fell right off it onto the deck below he was so frightened. He really hurt himself but they didn't care. They just made him do it again.'

He stopped.

Alfred put out his hand and gripped the boy's shoulder.

'The captain then steered the ship to a special place where there are lots of sharks,' said the boy. 'He knows all the seas there are. He can find his way in the dark in this ship and he even knows the haunts of the sea creatures. Anyway, when he found the right place he anchored the ship, all by himself, concentrating on every movement. Then he ordered one of the ship's monkeys to be

Chapter Fourteen

Alfred lay awake in the pirate ship listening to the conflicting snores from the heavy hammocks around him. A sailor cried out in his sleep like a child but he couldn't understand the words. There was a hiss out of the darkness, beckoning him. He slid out of his bedding and stepped barefoot along the deck, hesitant at first. It was the red-headed boy, he saw then, standing against the great hewn mainmast where it grew out of the floor like a shiny branchless tree, stretching up through the planks overhead. The ship dipped and creaked as they stood there, the bond strong between them.

'Hi,' whispered the boy.

'What's your name?' asked Alfred. It had not occurred to him to ask when they spoke before. 'Mine's Alfred.'

'Louis Oliver Boswell,' replied the boy. 'At least, that's what they called me at home. I don't need a name here. I can hardly remember what my real name is. They call me Louis Door sometimes; I don't know why.'

'Why aren't you asleep?' asked Alfred. His own voice had dropped to a whisper, imitating the other boy's.

'I wanted you to explore with me. I thought, maybe, we could try to escape.'

'What, in the middle of the ocean?' exclaimed Alfred. 'We'd never make it.'

'No, not *now*. But whenever we could. Later. There must be some chance to do it. When we are in port. But if the captain got wind of it, they'd put us in irons before we got anywhere near land. I thought we could look around the ship and see if we get any ideas. There are three decks. I was wondering ...'

'Yes?'

'Well, maybe when we are putting in for stores and water somewhere next time, we could hide. Perhaps they would forget about us when they are busy, and then at night maybe we could jump overboard and swim to shore.'

'Yeah,' agreed Alfred. 'Maybe we could. It's worth a try. But where would we go?'

In a funny way the ship was becoming home to him, he realised, now the question of escape had come up. He never noticed the rolling any more and the first mate, after all his instruction, had grown important to him. How long had he been here? He couldn't remember. Did he actually *want* to escape?

'Anywhere,' answered Louis. 'We'll die on this ship, else. For definite.'

Alfred said nothing, but followed the skinny form into the shadows.

'There's probably nowhere on the middle deck here. The captain's cabin' ... he shivered ... 'is at the back, behind us.'

'Yes,' said Alfred. 'I know. He had me in there for a little chat.'

'Ahead is the galley, right? There's nowhere to hide there, or aft. We'll have to look below in the hold. But if they catch us down there, that'll be it. Are you up for this?'

'OK,' replied Alfred. He supposed he ought to be afraid, but he wasn't. 'The ones down here are mostly asleep, anyway.'

'We'll have to pass by the cook to go down there.'

They moved like cats in the gloom, Louis in the lead. There was steam coming out of the galley and they could make out the giant figure of the cook, his back to them, doing something at his range. Both boys were hungry, as usual, but the cook wasn't the sort of character to slide them a titbit in the evening. He wasn't much of a cook at all, thought Alfred. Altogether the opposite of Long John – towering over the rest of the crew, and taciturn and morose – he was no fussier about hygiene than the rest of the pirates.

'I wonder what he's cooking,' said Alfred. The smell was unidentifiable.

'Curried rope, probably,' said Louis.

There was little light coming up from the hold. They went stealthily down the narrow steps. Alfred found that his heart was pounding again. It always was, these days. The heat from below and the stench were even worse. Louis stopped at the bottom step like a shadow. They waited, but there were no noises that suggested that crew members might be around. They crept forward. The lower deck had a series of storerooms, but all was dark.

'We need a candle,' said Louis.

'We'll set the ship on fire if we're not careful,' said Alfred. 'What about a lantern?'

Louis disappeared back upstairs and returned after about five minutes with a brass lantern tight against his chest. They began to investigate the storerooms. The first contained spare sails, neatly rolled in long bundles resting on wooden slats. As Louis raised the light, they could see rats scattering on the floor, their eyes gleaming in the beam. They seemed to have been gnawing the edge of one of the sails, which had been carelessly rolled.

'That's bad,' observed Louis. 'Un-seamanlike. Have to protect the spare sails. Can save your life sometimes.'

'Why?' asked Alfred. The confusion of billowing sails booming above seemed to him more than could ever be needed.

'The enemy can shoot holes in your sails easily. Pirates do it to victim ships to prevent them escaping. The same could happen to them, couldn't it? Or us. Sometimes they capture sails too. These probably come off other ships.'

Beyond were several rooms full of barrels.

'What's this – gunpowder?' asked Alfred.

'No, that's next door. This is all food and drink. Captured brandy and stuff. Bathfuls of beer. It's all locked up. Only the captain has the key. Normally he won't let the men have more than their daily rum, although they often seem to get drunk on that. He knows how to control them, though.'

There were endless barrels of salt- ed meat and flour. The drink barrels and bottles of wine were in a kind of wooden cage, padlocked as the boy had predicted. They were all tightly wedged together to prevent them from rolling about.

'Nowhere to hide here,' said Louis. 'No spare space.'

They wandered from room to room, the bread store, the carpenter's workshop, and other storerooms with chains and spare anchors. The only place seemed to be right under the spare sails. There was just enough room for the thinner boy to secrete himself.

'You know what,' said Alfred, 'your idea might work, but not for both of us at once. You could do it, while I cover for you. I could tell the mate you'd fallen overboard. I could do the lookout duty for you, and you could escape. Then I could try later.'

It wasn't a matter of being a hero. He knew somehow that he had to stay on board the ship; there was something he had to do. But Louis had his own destiny.

'Would you do that for me? I'd rather you came with me, though. We could stick together. Find our fortunes together.'

'Let's keep our eyes open,' said Alfred. 'At least we've got a sort of plan. You might have to decide quickly sometime. I'll help you. Whatever you do.'

They shook hands solemnly at the foot of the stairs.

'Will you go back to England?' asked Alfred.

Louis shrugged, his eyes fixed intently on Alfred.

'I don't even know where we are now. The Windward Islands maybe. Someone talked about them today. I think after this I would just stay in any country, anywhere I was. I'd become a priest. Or a steeplejack. I'm not afraid of heights any more, *I* can tell you.'

He froze. There was a shuffling noise from somewhere. Someone was coming. They withdrew silently into the dark, stepping away from the stairs and back towards the stores. It was one of the monkeys, roaming the passages in search of food. They watched him reach the stairs and climb nimbly above. Alfred laughed.

'Thought it was one of the captain's spies,' he said.

He looked at Louis. The boy was white-faced, his eyes large. He squeezed his arm.

'Be brave, Louis,' he said. 'We'll be OK. You'll see.'

Chapter Fifteen

Alfred's prowess with cutlass and dagger had never yet been put to the test, but the hours of demanding practice had given him a new skill and confidence, and the first mate had now begun to teach him some basic information about firearms.

For a whole week the ship had travelled short distances, this way and that, apparently at the whim of the captain. The reason, confirmed by Louis, was that they were lying in wait for a fat trader.

Normally they all woke at daylight. The morning arrived when Alfred awoke to a hand over his mouth. Silently he slipped from his hammock and followed the two or three pirates still below up to the main deck. It was dawn and the ship was shrouded in mist. It was drifting slowly and Alfred watched the captain, intent at the wheel like a snake for the kill, famished through long privation, but restrained and controlled until the right moment. The first mate spotted Alfred and beckoned to him.

'This is it, Alfredo. We've been following this plump chicken of a ship for two days, just out of sight, nudging forwards and backwards, just out of range. Now the captain has crept up on them in the night and we're right on top of them with this beautiful mist and flying the flag. He's a true master, the captain. Everything falls right into his palms, even the weather.' He hissed appreciatively.

Alfred felt sick with tension. What was he supposed to do? Warn the ship somehow? Jump overboard and swim away? He looked at the floor.

'Now, remember what I've taught you. You'll stand right beside me. When we touch their side, the boys will lash the capstans together in seconds so they can't escape. We and the rest will jump across, screaming for blood. Kill everybody you can reach as quickly as possible. Remember, once the blade is in, twist it round before you pull it out. And keep count, for your belt. Look!'

He pulled up his shirt to reveal a thick, worn belt covered with lines scored in the leather. He twisted round proudly and Alfred glimpsed the scars on his body.

'My total so far. As good as any man afloat, I'll wager you. You can count them later, should you be so minded, since we all know you have an interest in *numbers*. Ha ha! Perhaps today I'll be adding a few more to your books.'

He laughed again with the devil-may-care disregard that had so chilled Alfred two days before. He looked closely at the first mate. The man was taut to breaking point with excitement and danger, his lethal concentration like heat. He was a hunting dog on a leash, keyed up like the captain for the kill, scenting blood as acutely as any of the captain's sharks.

Alfred said nothing. He wished himself elsewhere with all his will, but the procedure had never proved successful in the past, and didn't now. He was, for some reason, not at all scared for himself but for what was about to happen to their victims. He had automatically accepted the proffered cutlass from the quartermaster and now stood in silence, his fingers clenched round the grip. The ship moved on remorselessly and innocently, as if approaching a peaceful harbour. The crew were silent to a man, each at their practised positions, a mixture of fearful weapons intently poised. Alfred caught sight of the captain again and looked quickly away. His face was drawn and somehow ecstatic, his body like a steel bar. He was half-crouched at the wheel, his head to one side like a musician tuning a difficult string, judging the moment to unleash his sea-wolves.

Suddenly there was a great bump and he nearly tumbled over. They were there, right alongside another, smaller ship, neatly length by length, and the hands flung their deadly ropes to trap their victim as firmly as would a giant spider. He saw the rest of the pirates, his fellow seamen, leap screaming and howling from their stations, some hopping over the rail, others leaping like winged devils from the rigging – all giving vent to an unearthly, terrifying cacophony. Despite himself, and somehow devoid of fear, Alfred shrugged and went after them. He vaulted over the rail and landed, looking for the first mate, clutching his cutlass.

There was already one body right at his feet, much blood about the neck where the head had virtually been cut right off. Alfred almost tripped over the legs. He looked down, trying to gauge the sailor's age. He seemed to be about sixteen.

'Too late, Alfredo, he's *mine*! And nearly off in one go!'

The mate was high above him in the rigging, fighting hand-to-hand exuberantly with a second sailor, his left hand behind his back. The mate forced the conflict higher and higher until the swords flashed in the sunlight above their heads, whereupon he lunged with his left hand holding his dagger and ran his opponent through the stomach, dragging the blade downwards.

The sailor fell heavily from the rigging and crashed to the deck. Alfred looked at his face. It was contorted with pain.

'All yours, Alfredo! On a plate. Your first, I believe?'

A high-pitched laugh came from above. Alfred looked again at the sailor. 'Can this be happening?' he wondered, 'can this really be …'

He cried out as a burning pain seared his upper thigh. The 'enemy' sailor was by no means already dead. He had reached up convulsively and stabbed at Alfred as hard as he could. Alfred looked incredulously at his wound. It was pouring blood but after the initial impact it didn't seem to hurt at all. He looked again at the wounded sailor. After the violent movement, his intestines were spilling out onto the deck. He felt no impulse at all to hit back at the wounded man, whose behaviour seemed to him quite forgivable.

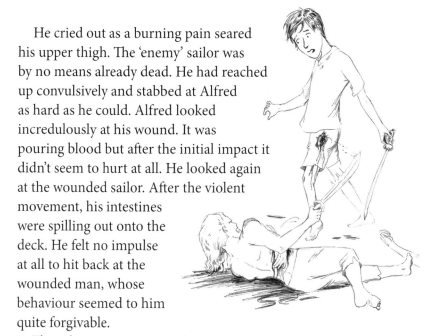

Then the captain, passing by, shot the man dead at close range.

'Get on with it you fool! Stamp them all out. Straight away. Like me!'

'And me,' cried the mate. He threw another dead sailor down onto the deck. 'Like *me* ...'

Alfred sat down. All over the ship the pirates were efficiently and merrily doling out death. The victim sailors had hardly been awake when the pirates fell on them and had no real chance to defend themselves. Blood ran again on the deck, as the boy had described, and the planks grew slippery and treacherous. *Where was Louis?* he wondered.

Most of the murder was quickly done. The captain and his second-in-command, their eyes shining, arms reddened to the shoulder, mounted a joint rush on the upper suite of cabins where the ship's captain was presumably still in his bunk. Two foolhardy sailors attempted to prevent their access and both died within seconds in a welter of bloody blows. The captain pulled up short.

'Get that pestilential scribe here. Perhaps there'll be something for him in there.'

Alfred, dazed and now in pain, was dragged up the steps by two pirates and presented for duty. The captain kicked open the cabin door. It had two delicately inlaid panels of coloured wood showing trees and a pair of peacocks. The panels splintered at once into fragments. The captain and the mate roared into the room. The merchant captain was still in his bed, sitting up in terror and unable to move.

'Where's your gold, scum?' demanded the pirate captain, boiling over with savagery. Spittle flew from his mouth. He was quivering.

The other captain looked at him.

'Where is your gold …?' repeated the pirate, softly.

The merchant captain got out of bed, stood up and spat on the floor. Instantly the pirates acted. The first mate seized him and forced his right arm flat down on the navigation table. The other pirate produced a deadly little axe from somewhere and without any hesitation at all chopped off his hand. It lay on the table, the fingers splayed on a sea chart.

'Think it over. You have some gold, somewhere, perhaps …?' said the deadly voice.

The captain looked at his arm and passed out.

'Alfred, get his keys,' said the mate, pointing to the bunch at the unconscious man's waist.

Despite himself Alfred did as he was instructed, but the keys were attached to a heavy belt and he couldn't get them off. While he held it conveniently, the mate cut it in two. The captain, meanwhile, practised at such things, had already located the safe. He threw back the heavy iron door. There was silence. The yield was poor, at least much poorer than anticipated. He scooped what there was onto the table, knocking the severed hand onto the floor as he did so. He kicked it out of the way but noticing a glint at the knuckles he told Alfred to take off the rings. The captain ran his own gory hands through the glinting coins.

'There must be more than this. It's a damned merchant ship, isn't it? Wake him up.'

The unfortunate merchant captain was dragged off the floor and tied upright in his own chair. Buckets of sea water were thrown over him until he recovered consciousness.

'Where is the gold?' repeated the pirate. He drew his dagger, slowly, and cut a thin red line right down the captain's face and neck. The captain struggled to concentrate.

'That's all we brought. Wages only. We're selling, this trip, not buying.'

'Selling what, scumbag?'

'Cloth. Textiles. *Venetian* textiles.' The captain closed his eyes.

The pirate leader swore a string of oaths. The first mate laughed.

'There'll be other things, captain. There always are. Shall we not go and look?'

'Impale this sickening toad on his bowsprit first. Then enjoy what's there to enjoy. Later there'll be fireworks. The boy scribe and I must find ourselves a *ledger* or two here.'

The merchant captain was untied from the chair and carried bodily outside. After a while there was an atrocious, persistent scream.

'They must have done something careless,' said the captain, and kicked the shattered door to with a laugh. He looked speculatively round the cabin, picking up things that he liked the look of, and piling them on the floor in a heap. The merchantman was not of the richest, but the sextant and compasses were of fine work, and there were other baubles that took the captain's fancy. He was not satisfied with the hunt, however; he was still bubbling with a hunger for violence and cruelty. Alfred judged that his own life hung by a thread, caged as he was with such an unpredictable killer. He found a leather-bound book marked *Accounts*, and opened it, thinking uncomfortably that the ship's captain would have been outraged at the intrusion. About one-third of the pages had already been used.

'Captain, I've found us a ledger. It will do perfectly.'

'Bring it here.' The pirate looked at the imposing folio sheets of manuscript calculations.

'You can read all that? Understand it?'

'Easily.'

Struck by a sudden idea, the pirate turned to the last inscribed page and pointed to the final entry.

'Does that tell you how much gold they have here on board?'

Alfred sat down at the table and put his head in his hands. There were various entries over the last two written pages from which he should be able to calculate the captain's total resources in gold when they had set out four days before. He scribbled some notes himself in the margin with the captain's quill, playing for time, and trying to look intelligent and reliable at the same time. He was rather taken aback at the speed with which the captain had realised the possibilities of the ship's account book. He reached his total and checked it twice for safety.

'What is it?'

Together they counted the gold that had been taken from the safe. The captain was quick at that, too. There was a large discrepancy.

'It must be here somewhere.'

The captain rapped round all the walls impatiently with the handle of his axe, growing increasingly restless. Alfred thought quickly. It occurred to him that perhaps there was another reason why the merchant captain had stayed put in bed.

'What about the couch, captain?'

'Could be. It's a common enough place. Take a look.'

There was a small, iron-bound chest shoved far under the bed, behind a porcelain chamber pot. It was closed with a padlock, but the padlock itself was not locked. They threw back the heavy lid. It was chock full of Venetian gold coins – it took much longer to count than the previous hoard. A dead man's chest, thought Alfred to himself, a dead man's chest. This time there was large discrepancy the other way: the captain had been carrying a good deal more gold than his books showed.

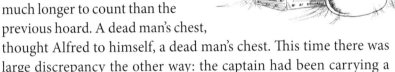

'A crafty skunk,' said the captain, appreciatively, 'but they're always loaded, these vessels. This extra will certainly please the boys.'

With the discovery of the second quantity of gold, the captain's mood lifted. Alfred was puzzled – clearly it did not occur to the captain to take the contents of the chest for himself. The pirate closed the lid.

'Right. Put all the goods together here. Anything you want, books, clothes, anything here, take it. Get your pestilential pens. The rule is, we share the gold out; anything else you must share out between you. Take everything valuable or usable that is movable. We'll make a pirate of you yet.'

On deck, the entire ship's crew seemed to be dead. The sun was now well up, and flies and wheeling seabirds had appeared, drawn by the grisly display of massacred sailors. Out of the corner of his eye Alfred caught a glimpse of what had befallen the other captain, and turned his back. The pirates, whistling or humming, were carrying

all manner of goods across the bulwarks to stow them safely in their own ship, stepping neatly over a body where one lay in the path. Flagons of wine appeared at that point and were distributed to all hands.

'Easy does it, now,' warned the captain. 'Let's finish the labour first. I want that ship on the bottom by the turn of the hour.'

Nobody really wanted the heavy bales of textiles, although they were ordered to take them, but there were cases of beautiful swords and razors which delighted all the pirates. Gradually the commotion died down. When everything useful was shifted on board, steps were taken to prepare for the sinking of the trader. The sails were lowered and taken off, and the masts felled by a frenzied attack with axes. The captain had decided to sink the ship with cannon fire, so the gunners went below to prepare their cannon.

The first mate stood watching while they untied the ropes that had held the ill-fated ship captive. Judging his moment, he stepped idly across and bent over the twisted shape of the seaman who, in his death throes, had stabbed Alfred. He made a couple of swift cuts and, at what seemed the last possible minute, jumped back, triumphantly brandishing a cluster of shiny guts over his head.

'Ideal bait, just excellent. Best possible quality.' He laughed with pleasure, the entrails rippling between his fingers.

Alfred fell to his knees on the deck, and vomited for all he was worth …

'Bring the bowl, Frederick, quickly! He's throwing up,' called Mrs Appletree. She held Alfred's head firmly until the nausea subsided and laid him back quietly on the bed.

'Another night of this and I'll be ill myself,' she said. 'Come on, Alfie boy, it's high time you got better …'

Chapter Sixteen

But Alfred, to his parents' delight, was clearly better the next morning. By then it was Thursday. He sat up in bed, and actually asked about breakfast.

'Whatever you fancy, Alfred,' said Mrs Appletree, drawing back the curtains. 'Just say the word. By the way, there is a letter for you. I have no idea who it's from.'

It was typewritten, with his name and address correct, but much larger than a normal envelope. He opened it carefully. There was a card inside, full of signatures and messages. The picture showed a game of football in progress. His form teacher, Miss Churchill, had written:

Dear Alfred,
We all miss you and are looking forward to your speedy return.
Very best wishes from us all.

There were about thirty variations on this theme, ranging from *Get well soon Alfie*, from about half the girls, to *We've nicked everything in your desk ha ha, Not dead yet Half-man?* and *Space Head*, from certain of his closer friends. Josephine had written *The weather is here. Wish you were lovely. Pathetic*, thought Alfred. He thought of how everybody had signed the plaster when Stephanie had broken her arm and felt rather grateful that they hadn't come round to scrawl their messages all over his pyjamas.

The next day he got out of bed for a few hours and by the weekend it did seem that he was beginning to get over what had been a very nasty thing.

'Bring him in for check-up in about a week,' had been Dr MacFarlane's parting shot on the Saturday morning, 'and we'll decide then whether it's the Foreign Legion for him or if he can go back to school.'

The magical return to the 'old Alfred', however, did not happen straight away. He was left weakened and listless and didn't seem to have sufficient energy to accomplish anything. The trouble was that he just couldn't seem to concentrate properly. Mrs Appletree brought him a pile of interesting library books that afternoon, but he wasn't in a 'reading mood', and other tactful suggestions over the next few days only established that he wasn't really in an 'anything at all mood'.

Alfred just mooched about. He drastically overfed the angel fish in his fish tank because they had been neglected while he lay ill. Barnacles or something seemed to be growing inside on the glass, but he couldn't be bothered to clean it out now. He gazed through into the depths. Nothing had changed. The grey-suited diver was still laboriously inspecting the miniature galleon on the bottom, surrounded by bubbles.

His mother, now she had stopped worrying, began to find Alfred's lying around the house and getting in the way a bit irritating, but the doctor had been adamant that he should recuperate fully before returning to school, and she tried to be patient. Preparing for bed that night she mentioned it to her husband.

'The boy needs distracting,' said his father, hunting for a mislaid slipper, 'something to take his mind off being poorly. Perhaps we should get an au pair?'

'Frederick! Really!' said Mrs Appletree.

A remark overheard at work the next day about a convalescent aunt and her jigsaws gave Mr Appletree a different idea, and during his lunch hour he went out to a nearby toy shop to invest in the largest puzzle he could find. He was lucky to be served by an assistant who took his question as a personal challenge and dug out the most up-to-date and complicated examples that he had in stock. One which he recommended had the whole surface of the picture filled by matchsticks, all lying this way and that.

'Should take a bright youngster a good few days,' he said.

Mr Appletree thought to himself that it would probably be more satisfying to turn the jigsaw right over and join up the plain cardboard backs instead. Something more stimulating was required for Alfred, something with an interesting picture that would be worth all the effort.

'We do have some more old-fashioned ones too,' said the shopkeeper, stooping to a lower shelf, 'with hundreds of pieces. There's a circus ring with ponies, a cricket match on a village green, and … a Spanish galleon, I think. Yes, here we are.'

He produced some dusty boxes for inspection. Alfred's father thought that the galleon would be most likely to appeal.

'Tell him to have a go without looking at the picture on the lid. Much more fun,' said the shopkeeper, tying string. 'You should always start with the edge and work inwards. Like drinking hot soup …'

Alfred greeted his father's parcel that evening with less enthusiasm than Mr Appletree had hoped, but he perked up considerably when the proud ship emerged from under the cellophane and the fine details of the painting were revealed.

'Wow. A thousand pieces,' said his mother, taken aback. 'How long will that take?' She smiled to see Alfred thoughtfully shaking the box.

'Oh, a good week for a beginner, I'd say,' replied Mr Appletree airily, 'maybe longer. We can't expect Alfie to do much in his condition.'

'Humph,' said Alfred. 'I'll start right after supper. Just watch the Master.'

Chapter Seventeen

It was a noble galleon, well equipped for battle with an offensive row of cannon poking out, primed to fight to the bitter end. It was years since Alfred had even thought about a jigsaw, but now he was absorbed, searching among the pieces to build up the picture: the spray as the prow dipped into the blue, the taut rigging straining with each movement. He worked for an hour and nearly completed the central mast, following the ropes down to the deck, hearing as he did so the creaking of the masts and spars and the bluster of the heavy sails in the wind far above his head.

His head drooped on his outstretched arm. In the peaceful silence of the house …

… the sea was flat under the hot sky and the first mate was talkative as they fished. He had fallen, unusually, into a reflective mood, and was speaking about his childhood. A nod or two from Alfred encouraged a stream of information.

'I did have a sister,' continued the mate, as if Alfred had contradicted him. 'We were twins, maybe we still are, somehow. But she died. Of blood in the lungs. Like they all did. There I was, you see, alone.'

Alfred was more interested to discover how he had become a pirate in the first place, or how he had got his terrible scars, but he didn't dare to interrupt.

'Took the King's Shilling, then I found myself on a ship, travelling the world, looking for adventure,' the mate remarked, twisting some tobacco in his pouch.

Alfred said nothing.

'Ran away, as you might say,' he continued, 'to sea.'

There was a pause. The mate began chewing, talking reminiscently, as if to himself.

'I went first to Portsmouth, like many a sailor lad before me. There was a dead pirate there covered in pitch, hung up as a warning. Frightened me rigid, I can tell you, that stiff in its year-round waterproofing. Little did I figure that I'd be a pirate myself before long. I've seen many a dead pirate since then, as we all have, but none with a smoking-suit that was such a good fit.'

He laughed, and looked up quizzically at Alfred.

'What happened then?'

'I signed up as one of the hands on a merchantman. I was one of those that they didn't need to press-gang. There were other boys like me, all needing to leave England for pastures new. We figured we could learn the ropes. Pull our own weight together. You know, boyo?'

Alfred nodded again. He was picking his teeth with a fishbone, a habit that he had unconsciously adopted from the mate.

'It wasn't so easy, mind you. Two of those boys were dead within a fortnight. One was flogged to death, the other drowned himself. We had picked a really bad ship. The master was a drunkard and a real killer. I decided to transfer my allegiance, as you might say, and deserted in the next port. I waited until the ship left and joined another. It was free and easy. I learned to sail and to navigate a little. And to fish.'

Alfred, reminded, tugged cautiously on his own line, checking it for resistance.

'I ended up on a full-blown sailing ship, serving before the mast with my fellow man. Got tough the hardest way, on hard work, terrible storms and dreadful food. On long voyages there was sometimes nothing to eat but biscuit and weevils, mostly weevils. But I found some good mates. You learn to think to yourself and keep your own counsel. No gambling. Watching the sea and the sky, moving with the water. You can learn a lot, watching the sea at night under the sweeping blackness.'

'Did you miss life on land?'

'Not for a minute. That was for God-fearing women and children. I wanted to stand on my feet and seek my fortune. Then my fortune changed with a bump. We were twice attacked by pirates on that fine ship. Things were never the same after that.'

'What happened?'

'Oh, the first time, nothing much. They got frightened off when another ship popped providentially over the horizon.'

He spat over the side.

'The second time was altogether a different story. They came right up alongside out of the deep blue. They were true professionals. They slaughtered half the hands straight off. While they were rampaging through the holds their captain stopped and asked me, just like that, if I wanted to join his crew instead. The funny thing was I wasn't at all scared. I'd never been in a battle or anything, but I wasn't at all worried about dying during the fighting. I just watched it all, fascinated. I'd never seen a dead man, apart from the one I mentioned, let alone one bleeding to death. Then, when he asked me, I agreed straight away. Better than going to the bottom, but anyway it seemed the most natural thing in the world for me to become a gentleman of fortune myself. I crossed right over the rail and joined his crew.'

'And then?'

'*Gold*. Lots of beautiful, heavy gold. There's nothing to compare with warm gold coins. Food and drink, and a shipful of adventure. Mind you, Alfredo, this was a big ship, with a lot of pirates. The captain had a habit of recruiting likely men as he went, and there were many other hands on board who'd been serving on law-abiding ships and been given the option like me. Often they had suffered such hardships with bad captains that they were only too glad to come over. But in the end, there were just too many hands to feed, and too many idle. One especially successful week we captured a sloop, disposed of its crew, and kept it. The captain fitted it out with extra supplies and arms, and appointed our captain here to take command of her. We swore oaths of allegiance to help one another at all times, stitched and hoisted our own Jolly Roger, and parted, with a tremendous squandering of explosives in celebration. We've never seen the other ship since, although someone heard she'd been sunk off the Azores. He was a great captain … taught me a lot … So here I am. And here you are.'

'And we can never go home.'

'Home? I'd never care to, myself. But, you know, I've heard that sometimes they announce pardons for pirates who do want to retire. Perhaps you'll end up yet with a full belly and a big house full of children. Me, I'd rather go down to the bottom in fire and bloodshed. Then the fish can get their own back on me for a change. I'll never go back to life on land.'

The mate went below. Alfred gazed out over the horizon. The sun threw a haze on the water and there were no sharp lines anywhere. He fell into a reverie, secretly homesick for England, and dry land, and home …

Alfred awoke, chilled and uncomfortable. He cleaned his teeth and fell into bed as quickly as possible.

Chapter Eighteen

Alfred yawned like a whale among his pillows and looked at his watch. It was 6.13am. Normally he would never be awake at such an hour, but he felt inexplicably lively. His father and mother would still be in bed, he thought, as there was no sound from below. He put on his dressing gown and wandered over to the table where he had made a start on the jigsaw the day before.

Despite his boast he had not yet accomplished much. Completing the edges had been easy enough, but moving in from there was not so simple: there was blue sky above and blue sea below, and not much to distinguish the two. He decided to leave that till later and start work on the body of the ship in the middle. He yawned again, slowly, more like a waiting crocodile just below the water …

They did have a parrot on board after all, he discovered, going below decks himself again. It was old and dusty, and looked at him with jaded cynicism. The parrot lived in a cage below and refused ever to go out into the fresh air or sunshine. It preferred an atmosphere of gloom and tobacco smoke, and had spent so much time watching the hands play cards or dice that it was an expert gambler. The parrot was female and called Vera because she always told lies, according to the first mate.

'Ello Ve-ra,' said Alfred, experimentally. He had the oddest feeling of having said that before. The parrot grimaced at Alfred with undisguised loathing and spat expressively on the floor.

'*Charming*,' said Alfred.

'Same to you, Fish-face,' said the parrot in a broken croak, and turned its back.

That parrot was not the only wildlife aboard. There were still several monkeys left, as they'd discovered the other night, as well as a small ape and the ship's cat, Cleo. The monkeys, and especially the ape, were into everything with their crafty fingers and all over the place. Louis had told him how one morning before Alfred had arrived, the captain had shot two monkeys dead on the spot and handed them by the tails to the cook, saying laconically, 'for the soup.'

It stank below. Appallingly. He wondered that the smell had not troubled him before, but supposed he just hadn't noticed when he was ill or constantly frightened. Even now two gamblers were below decks, intent on their dicing.

There was an oily cloth marked off in sections with what seemed to be a crown or an anchor drooped over a barrel. The two pirates tossed the dice intently, scattering the wagers heaped over it. There was a muttered dispute and one scooped up the coins with a low laugh. The other swore and stumbled up the companionway above decks, obviously the worse for drink …

Louis was down there now, chatting to the gunners. Between their nefarious engagements and other distractions they attended carefully to the cannon, cleaning the tools and even polishing the barrels. It reminded Alfred of … what? Of his father polishing his car on the forecourt of their house.

The silent weapons on their prehistoric wheels waiting for a summons fascinated both the boys. One or two were inappropriately handsome, with patterning and a crest. Louis told him that they were booty from other ships, even a man-o'-war. Pirates took anything they could use, even cannon that had been fired against them if they were superior. The chief gunner, Ferris, had long before been trained by the navy. 'Pinch the guns, pinch the gunners,' said Louis, surprisingly, and it dawned on Alfred that Louis hankered to be a gunner himself, although it was obvious that the hands would never be able to take him seriously. They had to be solid men, and strong, able to control their iron servants together.

'Wait till you hear a broadside,' said Ferris, 'you come down here next time. Watch the skirmish through the portholes.' He wound the oily rag back round his temples. 'Turn the ship about and fire the whole lot together! Phew! No air in here but black and gunpowder. No sound but the roar of death in thunderous unison. And the poor broken devils over the water, going down, and down.' He grinned, like they all seemed to at the idea of death, showing broken teeth.

'But,' said Jordan, the second gunner, 'we are artists when we have to be. Take out one mast, says the captain – that's what we do. Hole the sails, that's what we do. We're his personal cutlasses down here. His instruments.'

'Gunpowder, reason and shot,' thought Alfred inconsequentially, seated on a precarious pyramid of cannon balls. They were cleverly stacked, stable and within reach in a hurry. He half-wanted to ask them to fire off a cannon now, just for a demonstration, but that wasn't a proposal you could put to a professional pirate in the middle of the morning. There were other irons lying about, too, ball and chain and things that looked like dumbbells. Did they fire those too?

Louis feels best down here, he thought. This is where he must have been during the battle. Out of the way, near the big fighters, a sparrow with the rhinos …

Alfred rubbed his eyes. He had stupidly knocked a good part of what he had done of the jigsaw over the edge of the table. Some of it was recoverable, and he was nearly back where he had been before when his mother came in, yawning in her old pink dressing gown.

'Listen, Alfie, Dad has taken a day off and wants to take us out somewhere in the car. A country house, or somewhere. It will do you good. Let's have a quick breakfast and go. Gosh, you've done *lots*. What a super picture that is. You can almost imagine being on board, can't you?'

Chapter Nineteen

The rest of that time 'off' school just dragged. Alfred spent hours staring into space, apparently listening to something on his headphones, lying on the floor of his room, scribbling on bits of paper, and rereading parts of his old books. He hardly went out and didn't say much to anybody. He had been left alone now by the pirates for some time, but it was not reassuring. At the back of his mind, somewhere where he couldn't quite get it in focus, he knew he was waiting for something to happen.

'Alfred, you've got a visitor,' called Mrs Appletree on the Friday afternoon, from the front door. 'Will you come down?'

There was a drumming of feet on the stairs and Josephine charged into the room. She was horribly healthy and windswept, bringing a rush of energy with her that made Alfred feel dizzy.

'Alfie! I thought I'd come and check that you're really still alive. People are saying that you have been struck down by unknown *lurgies*, or run away to sea. I've just been playing tennis in the park with Mandy. She can't serve for toffee. It's hardly worth playing really, but it's good practice. I suppose you're too *decrepit* to go outdoors today?'

'We could go round the block?'

'Don't overdo it, Alfred. A little stroll down to the garden gate and back will be enough. We don't want to take any risks with our health, do we?'

'Do I still look delicate?'

'Weedy is the word. All this sickroom stuff is not what we need, Alfie boy. What's *wrong* with you anyway?'

'I don't know. You brought me home, doing your Florence Nightingale act. I'm surprised you haven't sent your diagnosis to the GP.'

'I need to check your records. So when are you coming back to school, then?'

'Actually, probably next week. We're supposed to see the doctor in a day or two, and he will probably say Monday.'

'You mean all this sympathy is wasted? Good thing I didn't buy any *grapes* or anything.'

'You'd have eaten them all yourself anyway.'

'True. They want me to write your obituary for the school magazine.'

'Check your spelling. Don't forget my prize.'

'For hypochondria, you mean? I *do* miss you, Alfie. Carrying my own bag home from school everyday, and everything. Having to buy chewing gum. Why are you so transparent-looking anyway?'

'I dunno. Not eating all my greens.'

'It'll end in spots, Sunbeam. Come on, let's go down to the river. You can always lean on my arm if you need to.'

'You're all heart.'

Chapter Twenty

He was back. No choice involved. No overture on his own part. He just was.

They were racing in the fading light up the rigging, their feet like spiders on the 'ratlines' as Louis insisted on calling them. Then the other boy was above him, nimbler on the ropes, and he was first to the lookout post. There was room for them both inside.

'I prefer it up here,' said Louis, 'even when I'm not on duty.'

'Yeah. It's safer, somehow. Even though you could easily fall on the way up. And it's cold.'

'Not really. If you're careful.'

'Are there any of the crew that you like?'

'Apart from the gunners? Not really. Some are more dangerous than you could imagine. One or two aren't so bad. Like the surgeon. He was a real ship's doctor once, till they snatched him off another ship. They're always on the lookout for useful crew. When they have to choose between death and joining up they usually join up. He never says anything, but I am not scared of him. And he does try and save lives. He patches up this crew as if they were real people. And cuts off bits if he needs to.'

'Bits?'

'Arms or legs that have been shot. In their battles. I had to help him last time, saw off a leg that couldn't be kept.'

'Just like that?'

'Yeah. They filled the sailor with rum and just sawed it off, holding him down together. Then there's the bit with the hot pitch. That's even worse. The very smell of pitch makes me sick now, when it's hot. The planks stink of it. That pirate died anyway, after a day or two. The carpenter never needed to carve him a leg.'

Alfred was silent.

'I suppose they all die young in this line of work.'

'Few get to die of old age. Many hang. And none go to Heaven.'

'That's for sure.'

They grinned at one another. Louis produced a paper containing some biscuits.

'I nicked these from the galley when the Minotaur wasn't looking.'

They munched. Soon they would need water.

'Hey, Alfie, have you served on many ships?'

'Er … no. Not really.'

'I thought so. But you'll get used to it. Another thing, you be careful of the first mate.'

'He's not so bad. I think he likes me.'

'Maybe he does. But according to the doctor he killed your predecessor and mine. With a handspike.'

'You're kidding. Why?'

'No idea. Probably broke his fishing line or something. They're all mad, I tell you. Killers all. What shall we do together when we've escaped?'

It was his favourite subject. He always seemed to come back to it.

Chapter Twenty-One

Most people who write about pirates have never actually met one, wrote Alfred. He fingered the scar on his leg, or at least where there ought to have been a scar. It seemed to have healed completely. It was important to get the thing right, now he had actually started. That was just the problem. Starting. He began again.

What do we really know about pirates?

He stared out of the window and gnawed at his wrap-around dollar banknote pencil. The task before him seemed impossible. The pages of notes he had made in the library, before his illness, seemed to have been written by somebody else; he could hardly read or understand them at all. It was clear from the books that he had consulted that mountains of facts were known about pirates, at least, to some people – far more than he could either control or summarise for his essay. His original plan seemed ludicrously ambitious. 'Perhaps I should think of something quite different,' he wondered.

When he let himself, he also got quickly into a panic about what he must be missing at school and all the sackfuls of homework he would have to do. Another thing was he had no idea how long the written part of a history topic was supposed to be. He looked up the Foreign Legion in the family encyclopaedia which was still lying about on the floor of his room. It seemed to have a lot going for it as an alternative to school. He went down into the hall for the telephone.

'Hello?'

'Ally-Pally! Can I be of assistance? Need a new vomit bag?'

'Not tonight, Josephine. How long are these blasted history topics supposed to be?'

'Mine is about 1000 words *so far.*'

'Mabe, you're a creep. A classic example of creephood.'

'Once you get started … anyway, Mum let me use her computer. It counts the words that you've done. Just put down lots of *ands* and *its*. Shall I write some for you? It is supposed to be about ten pages altogether, with drawings or illustrations, Williff said.'

'So what are you writing about?'

'That's a classified secret.'

'Utter double creep.'

He sat at his desk, trying to visualise how one thousand or even five hundred words would look if they were already written on his sheets of paper. He just couldn't imagine it, he discovered.

Perhaps he should rough out some of the illustrations for his pirate essay since he was having such trouble with the writing? He had always been good at drawing. Somehow, though, his pencil would only produce death. He tried to draw the first mate as he looked when he was fishing on deck, but the figure just wouldn't work. It was lifeless, out of proportion and had nothing recognisably to do with pirates. He tried a quick sketch of the same character triumphant in the rigging, stabbing down at his enemy, and there was a sudden, shocking life in the picture. Could he put *that* in his school essay?

Josephine had made one useful suggestion. It was time to ask his mother if he could use her computer. As he went downstairs Alfred heard her 'instruction' voice from the front room, high and firm above the background music. The door happened to be ajar. She was leading one of her groups:

'Stre-e-etch those fingertips just as far as you can: str-e-etch …'

'Re-e-etch, you wre-e-etch …' thought Alfred to himself.

The ladies in their leotards were fearless and confident. They could probably deal with a boatload of angry pirates without any trouble at all, he thought. There was faint but attractive sunlight playing outside, and he felt unable to stay indoors a moment longer. He went downstairs and wandered into the garden to look for a frog.

'I just don't know what's the *matter* with that boy,' said Mrs Appletree to her husband that evening. 'It's high time he was back at school. He's never going to get his strength back flopping about the house. I think on Monday it will be time.'

Mr Appletree grunted. He was deep in a mountaineering book.

Chapter Twenty-Two

Saturday was not a good day after the cross-off-the-list visit to the doctor's. There was now no escape from school and all that meant. Alfred was grumpy and out of sorts. His parents were busy about their own affairs and he was left to his own devices, which was probably a good thing. He lay on the grass at the back under the trees, reading chunks of an old comic book. It was painful after a while. He rolled over with his hands behind his head and stared up at the sky through the branches ...

For the first time, they were going ashore. The ship was deftly anchored in a bay to the south of the island, although Louis said there were other spots suitable for a lengthier berth: they obviously used the island regularly. Now they needed water badly, as well as fresh fruit and meat. Three crew members and the captain stayed aboard while the remainder went ashore under the command of the quartermaster.

The boats rowed ashore together in practised concentration. All of the pirates were armed, on their guard, taking nothing for granted, despite the familiarity of the island. They were nippy, the boats, breasting the surf and spilling the gaudy figures onto the sand. The water detail was very committed, marching their improvised cart with the first load of barrels at once up over the beach towards the greenery, but the others were greeted by a motley crowd of local people who poured out onto the beach, and there was laughter and shouting. The quartermaster was quickly negotiating for other supplies, including two or three extra sheep to be roasted there and then on the beach for everybody.

The boys were told to collect driftwood from the beach, and whatever else they could find, to start the great bonfire. Some of the island boys came to help them and soon there was a gang dragging the whitened trunks together, the lack of shared language no obstacle.

It was a party – there was no other word for it. Music was coming from somewhere; small drums, and some kind of flute, a lasting meandering melody, conjured out of the air by three or four men seated on the rocks. Before long the flames from the great pyre of dry wood began to lick upwards into the haze. The sheep had been readied and impaled, and were now turning delicately on improvised spits. Many of the pirates had brought baubles and other pretty things for the girls; it was clear that there were old friends among them, Alfred noticed. The tempting aroma of the cooking meat began to make him feel faint with hunger. It would be a long wait, though. The boys ran along the sand to explore the caves.

A solitary rowing boat creaked slowly out of the darkness and beached at some distance from the great beacon bonfire. It was the captain, come to join his men at the feast. Despite the closeness of the night he was sumptuously dressed. He walked across the sand with great deliberation, a braided coat thrown across his shoulders. There was a ripple of response from them all – not silence exactly, but a toning down of noise and exuberance. The headmaster coming into assembly, thought Alfred. The captain was followed by one of the crew, Josiah, carrying a chair. This was placed carefully on the sand at the far end of the fire area. They could see the captain seated with a straight back, declining meat, but accepting a deep vessel of the local drink offered to him by a cluster of the older men of the island. The first mate and the quartermaster were there at his right and left. There was an air of discipline about them that contrasted oddly with the celebrations all around them. They were more like ambassadors than vagabonds, thought Alfred, almost representing the Queen, with all the power of the navy behind them.

The boys themselves had gorged on the fragrant meat until they could hardly move. Alfred's lips and palate were burnt from the first mouthful, but he was happy. It had been a long time since either of them had eaten such food, and Louis actually looked a bit fatter. They would sleep ashore of course; none of the pirates was going anywhere. There were certainly animal noises from inland, grunts and snarls and even a distant howl, but neither of the boys was nervous. The fire was still sufficient to deter predators, and anyway one of their shipmates would be on watch. They lay talking quietly under the stars.

'Can you swim, Alfie?'

'Yeah. About four lengths, I guess.'

'*Lengths*?'

'Er – say, once round the whole ship. Four times round. Maybe.'

'We'll go tomorrow. The pirates won't swim in the sea. They think it's stupid.'

'I guess the sea is their enemy?'

'Maybe …'

Louis fell silent. Alfred lay in the hot night. There was no wind, so the smoke rose straight into the darkness. He could make out indistinct but enthusiastic singing below them on the shore. It was warm and he was very drowsy, on an island in the middle of a tropical sea. He slid into deep sleep …

… Josephine was there. It was a very hot afternoon. They were in his parents' garden. Alfred was doing something in the shed, moving something heavy. He had an anxious feeling about it. Where was it supposed to be? Josephine was down the far end, talking with her usual animation to someone on the other side of the fence. He couldn't see who it was. He had Josephine's birthday present ready somewhere. Where was it? Whom was she talking to? Looked like some boy he didn't know …

Louis woke him abruptly. It was just light and he was bruised from the inhospitable ground they had chosen.

'There's a waterfall,' said Louis, 'not far away. Let's go and jump in. It's great. Not salt.'

They slipped away from the sleeping forms that lay at odd angles, some covered, others fallen just as they were, dead to the world. They set off into dense undergrowth, Louis in the lead. He was a different boy altogether – excited and confident. Alfred was still a bit sleepy, but he followed carefully. It was a pirate island, after all, and here he was walking across it. Who knows what secrets lay scattered around or buried? Treasure. Small arms. Maps and stuff. God knows. Shouldn't they be looking for all that?

Louis stopped and bent to the ground, crouching immobile. Must at least be the hand of a skeleton, sticking out of the ground and pointing, thought Alfred. Louis stood triumphantly, his hands clasped together. He opened one palm gently to reveal a giant exotic grasshopper, delicate and trembling, pausing as if awaiting orders. He laughed and clucked the insect under what would be its chin if it had a real chin, so it leaped away into the ferns.

'It's through here,' called Louis, 'where they fill the barrels' – and indeed the rush of water could suddenly be heard.

They broke through beside a stream at the bottom of a green-covered cliff; the water poured in an arch from above, crashing with a dramatic rush into the green pool below. The boys tore off their shipboard togs and jumped as one into the coolness. There was simply too much water for splash fights. They crouched under the curtain of water, laughing and gasping, being flying fish. All of a sudden, Louis went rigid.

'What is it?' asked Alfred, making rude hippo noises.

'Gunfire,' said Louis. 'It's the summons from the ship.' He was out of the water and dressing in an instant. Alfred struggled, soaking wet, to get into his things and ran after his friend.

The beach was a great mess. The pirates were all up and gone; the last of them was wading out to the second jollyboat. The boys raced across the hot sand and into the sluggish lapping water. The pirate at the tiller laughed and Alfred thought in panic that they would be left behind. Why should they care, though? Couldn't they just stay on the island? Then, Louis cried out and nearly fell; he had cut his foot on something in the water. Alfred made a superhuman lunge and got them both within reach. They were pulled aboard by one of the gunners. Most of the pirates were drinking from coconuts and shells bobbed on the current as they pulled away. Play was over: duty called.

Chapter Twenty-Three

On that Saturday afternoon, Josephine reckoned she had completely finished her own topic and was ready to print it. That just left the pictures, and she felt she had those under control. She then had had a really good idea. Why not go with Alfred to see a film? They could go on the bus, she pointed out on the phone, more or less door to door.

'Come on Allie, it will do you good.'

'OK, but I'll probably fall asleep. I seem to be tired the whole time.'

'I'll buy you popcorn in a bucket. Nobody ever fell asleep eating popcorn.'

They waited a long time for the bus. Alfred was very quiet but Josephine was babbling away so it didn't matter. There weren't two seats together, so they decided to stand. Gradually the bus drew nearer to the town centre, but then it stopped, surrounded by traffic. They remained stationary for so long that people looked up from their newspapers or conversations and tut-tutted irritably, straining their necks to see what was going on and making intolerant remarks.

'Let's get *off*, Alfie,' suggested Josephine, 'it's not far to walk from here, and if we're not careful we'll miss the advertisements.'

Alfred followed her off the bus and onto the pavement. The traffic was locked solid and was obviously destined to remain so.

'It must be an accident,' said Josephine, and indeed the truth of that statement became evident as they went along. An ambulance was struggling the other way coming towards them, against the flow of the traffic. As they reached the post office they came to the scene itself. A cyclist had been hit by a car. The driver was striding about, his head in his hands, reeling from the impact and whimpering to himself, but nobody was looking after him at all. Several people were crouched in the road near the bent bicycle and as they came abreast of them Josephine caught sight of the injured rider, one arm thrown out protectively above his head, his thin body broken and still, silhouetted against the bright blood that flowed across the road. The body was obviously that of an adolescent, thin and browned. He seemed to have red hair, she thought.

By her side Alfred gasped and dashed into the road. He stood unmoving by the body with staring eyes, rigid with shock. She came up next to him.

'Come on, Alfie, we can't do anything,' but he looked at her in horror, without recognition, and she was quite unable to account for the severity of his evident suffering.

'Come, Alfie,' she whispered again, 'let's go home.'

He followed her without a word, but as they made their way slowly home from the bus stop in the gathering dusk she was startled to observe that he was crying. She said nothing at all, but softly took his hand in hers.

By the time they reached Josephine's house Alfred seemed to have recovered. She made him come in with her for cocoa, but he was glad that no-one asked why they were back so early. What was obviously Josephine's essay lay on the kitchen table. It looked very neat and professional from a distance, but she whisked it at once out of the room: no-one was allowed to look at it. She talked easily as usual, playing something noisy on the radio and finding a tin of biscuits, but she was watching him carefully when he wasn't looking.

Alfred, at the same time, was wondering if he could tell Josephine about Louis and the pirates, and what had been happening to him during the recent nights. How could he possibly begin? She would think he was mad. 'Every night I go somewhere else while you and all our friends are quietly asleep in bed.' But he didn't actually *go* anywhere, did he? And not every night, but it was pretty regular, now. He never knew when it would happen. And he had a friend over there. Even a sort of life there. He might even *belong* there, crazy though it sounded.

In the end he said nothing. He couldn't. She *would* think he was mad.

'So, am I mad then?' Alfred later spoke the question aloud, his nose pressed against the mirror in the bathroom. Could be, kid, he thought. His father always swore blind that Alfred's grandfather on the other side was batty, and everyone knew that insanity did run in families, but that was something different. Grandfather hoarded newspapers and milk bottles and took a very long time to answer questions, but otherwise he could pass for normal as far as Alfred could remember. But on the other hand, he himself could probably

pass for normal. No-one would guess about his secret life by night, would they? It would be alright. Once it had run its course, it would stop.

So he wasn't mad after all then? Just the victim of some freak event? Yeah, probably.

Nothing happened that night until the early hours. But the minute he was drawn back on board, he knew that something was badly amiss. What could have happened while he was away? Spray shot off the bowsprit as he stood nervously near the front of the ship, out of sight, gazing at the horizon that lay stretched infinitely before him. Something had gone terribly wrong.

Louis was dead.

There was his body, stretched out on a sail, lying on the deck.

The captain, a pirate told him as he stood there, had ordered Louis to be hung upside-down from his crow's nest for two days and nights because he had fallen asleep while they were following another victim, and they had missed their chance. The captain was so maniacally angry about it that no-one dared speak to him, not even the second-in-command. When eventually the mate dared to climb up and cut the boy down he was long dead and cold.

Alfred gazed in silence at the thin browned body on the deck. He couldn't take his eyes off his lifeless companion. Obscurely, behind his grief, he felt responsible. He had reassured Louis more than once that he would be safe, and he absolutely hadn't been. And yet he felt instinctively that if he had been on board at the time it wouldn't have happened that way. He knelt down to touch the boy's forehead. They would have been friends always. And now the hidden locket would stay hidden for ever. What must he have suffered, alone in his endless torture, bound like a mad pendulum above the ship in the dreadful cold and the dark? He had probably hoped that Alfred would come to rescue him when the others had forgotten. He felt burning tears about to come as he knelt by the slender corpse, one rigid skinny arm twisted above the head as if flung out in supplication. It was badly bruised. The cut on his foot had been a bad one. Louis would never escape now.

Again, the mate was watching him without his realising it.

'Consider yourself lucky, Alfredo my boy. If he'd found you at the time, you'd have been strung up there too. Where were you, anyway?'

Chapter Twenty-Four

All in all, therefore, Alfred was glad to get back to school that Monday, even though there was sarcasm to be swallowed from certain people about his 'holiday'. Distraction from private thoughts was crucial. Things had gone so far that there was now no-one with whom he could possibly talk. He was forced to mourn his lost friend in secret in a suddenly busy world where no-one even knew of the boy's existence. He tried not to think of Louis, dead on the deck. They would have thrown him overboard, of course. Not much of a meal for any fish.

On top of that, he was under major league pressure at school. He had missed a frightening amount of schoolwork, as well as having a mountain of new homework. He negotiated the loan of books from others in his class – including Adam, who was embarrassed, and Josephine, who wasn't – to copy up what he had missed. Josephine had terrible handwriting and, as he was to discover, didn't seem to be as attentive in lessons as she looked from the outside.

It was difficult to find out the truth about how far the others had progressed with their projects, too. It was like exams: people who said they had 'done terribly' or 'hadn't even completed the answers' usually got the best marks. He had the horrible idea that he might be the only person in the class who hadn't even properly *begun* writing. He decided that the time had come for the big push. 'Copy all this up,' he thought, 'and then I shall finish the first page if it kills me.'

The best days of your life ... he thought ruefully to himself, stuffing an overburdened backpack. What a *road* of *lubbish* ...

He worked hard trying to decipher Josephine's handwriting most of the evening, and tackled a bit of understandable maths homework. It was late when he turned to his pirate file. He was getting a bit further by avoiding page one, writing without thinking, describing shipboard life and trying to blot out Louis from his mind as he wrote.

It was silent in the house; his parents were below in the front room, but making no noise. He couldn't even hear the television. The room itself was dark, but his desk lamp threw a bright light on the papers. Alfred needed to check the correct words for ship fittings. He began to feel drowsy and felt his head begin to nod gently. He was startled by the sudden creak of a floorboard in the hall beyond his open door. He knew that treacherous spot of old and exactly how it was best avoided. It had creaked now precisely as if someone unfamiliar with the house had stepped on it for the first time.

He looked up, his ears straining. There was silence for a while. Then he thought he heard laughter. Laughter from a distance. It was cold, though, not friendly. Detached and merciless.

He sat with his chin in his hands. 'Perhaps I've got writer's cramp,' he thought to himself. He flexed the fingers of his right hand experimentally, but there was no noticeable ache. 'Or doodler's cramp?'

Again he heard a distant cackle of savage laughter. Alfred swung round in his seat and looked over his shoulder. He had a rather smart chair – a professional typist's chair – that rotated and also went up and down when a lever was brought into play. It used to belong to one of the secretaries in his father's bank and was going to be thrown away when the offices were refurbished. Mr Appletree had found it outside on the pavement and brought it home in the car for his son. He had fixed on the back an old metal shield inscribed *AA* which he found in the garage, so that everybody would know whose chair it was. Alfred always liked swivelling to and fro while doing his homework. It helped him to concentrate.

He stared into the shadows behind him, but there was nothing there.

Chapter Twenty-Five

After a day or two of hard work, the pirate file was no longer so slim, but the contents did not yet add up by any means to an essay that could be handed in to satisfy Mr Willoughby.

Alfred was trying to tackle an insuperable difficulty: if he wanted to he could now describe pirates clearly and convincingly, in contrast with the descriptions in the usual romantic stories, but how, as a 'historian', was he to explain his own knowledge of them?

Pirates in our day have a very inappropriate reputation, he wrote.

People think they were heroes. Their carefree lives, bravely fighting against stronger forces, snatching their gold in glamorous, daring raids, make us think of them with a warm glow of excitement. It's rather like successful gangsters today, or professional soldiers. People seem to forget the crime, or the killing, confused by a strange glamour. But pirates were, for the most part, just dangerous criminals …

Alfred gazed into space and worried over his notebooks. His head slid forward until his chin was resting thoughtfully on the open encyclopaedia. The lamp shone directly on his hair, illuminating it as if a halo.

Two pirates stood together in the doorway.

'I know you're there,' said Alfred, suddenly, 'both of you. There's no point in hiding. I'm not at all frightened of you here. This is *my* territory.'

But he *was* frightened. He sat rigid, willing them to go away and leave him alone. He stared defiantly into the shadowy corner of the

room, straining to make out their shapes. He thought he saw some movement in the corner of his eye, and the glint, or half-glint, of what could be a *blade*.

'If you think you can affect here, you're wrong. I know what's real and what isn't. You just aren't. This room is real, the desk is real, I'm re...'

He stopped, holding onto the edge of his chair. One of the pirates had laughed. There was no pretending otherwise. There was a long silence. Alfred suddenly wanted to go to the toilet, but he couldn't move. He thought he heard one of them say:

'We'll be back, writer boy ... we'll be back ...' and then he knew that they had gone.

He stayed clenched up for a long time. He could hear the blurred murmur of the television news programme below, and, intermittently, the faint sound of his parents talking, his mother laughing suddenly. He knew with the going-to-school and doing-a-chemistry-lesson part of his mind that there can have been no pirates in his room, but he needed desperately to do something familiar. He got up stiffly from the desk. He decided to go downstairs and find a glass of milk in the kitchen.

The stairs were in darkness. His mother was always turning lights off, complaining about electricity bills, but Alfred knew the stairs by heart and had often experimented with moving round the house with his eyes closed.

The light seemed brilliant in the white-tiled kitchen. He had known everything in it for his entire life. Alfred decided to make some hot chocolate instead. He stood absently by the stove, heedless of the bubbling milk. His mother came running in from the front room, followed by his father, alarmed by the burning smell.

'What are you *doing* Alfie? What a mess! You should have asked me to make it for you …'

'There's no use crying over burnt milk, dear. Actually, hot chocolate is a good idea. Why don't I make some more, for all of us?'

'It's OK guys, I'll clean it up,' said Alfred. He said nothing else to his parents, but he was more than glad of their company.

Half an hour later Alfred was talking to himself – not that he knew it – locked in the upstairs toilet. He sat like a statue. He was frightened, now. Truly. Dreaming of pirates was one thing. Seeing them and speaking to them in his own family house was something different. More like hallucinations or seeing ghosts. Maybe they *were* ghosts? But why were they *here*, and what had they got to do with *him*? And you could see through ghosts: they walked through walls and things. His pirates weren't dead anyway; they were more solid and real than … than dustmen. Actually, one of their regular dustmen looked a bit like a pirate; he always wore a tight scarf around his head and he certainly had tattoos on his forearms. At least with dreams, part of your mind knew you were dreaming, and that, sooner or later, you would wake up. Had he had that feeling on board the ship?

No, not really, and he was sometimes away for days on end. Maybe he *was* insane. He tried to imagine himself in a small room with bars and padding, with white-coated doctors pointing at him to one another and talking about 'delusions' and 'fixations'. He would have to get somebody's attention and talk about it. It was totally impossible that dead pirates could walk up his parents' staircase, wasn't it? He must be imagining them. OK so it was all in his imagination. *Fine.* No problem, then.

But they said they were coming back.

Chapter Twenty-Six

'A funny thing happened to me at work yesterday,' said Mr Appletree, looking up from the morning paper. 'Really made me think. You can never tell about people.'

Alfred was reading the side of the cereal packet for the millionth time about riboflavin and niacin.

'My deputy, Mr Bigelow,' said Mr Appletree, 'I think he might be mad.'

'Aren't all bankers certifiable?' asked Alfred's mother. 'Why worry now?' She got up to refill the teapot.

'This is extreme. The fellow plays with little toy soldiers. Not proper ones, like Alfie's, but microscopic. All over the floor. It must kill his knees. He has ancient battles all over the spare bedroom and fights them out with his chums in the evening. He's over fifty!'

'Perhaps he enjoys it,' said Mrs Appletree. 'How do you know about it? Has he invited you to be a general?'

'He had a new set of infantry arrive in a packet on his desk. Came in the post. I noticed it and asked if it was for one of his nephews.'

'Maybe you should try it, dear. Might be good exercise.'

'But the thing is, he told me he knew all about the battle because he was *in it once himself.* With Wellington. He knew I was interested in Napoleonic history, so he told me.'

'You must be kidding,' said Alfred. 'In a former life or something?'

'Apparently. He says he was in the military professionally. A brigadier or what have you. Remembers all about his earlier incarnation.'

'Do you have ex-pharaohs or Roman emperors working behind the counters then?' queried Mrs Appletree, lightly.

'Who knows? I guess most of these characters keep their out-of-the-body lives to themselves. Maybe the world is full of these nutcases. But to think that he's my deputy, and on the Board!'

'The thing with reincarnation, 'said Mrs Appletree, 'is that people are not supposed to be able to remember their earlier lives. If you can't remember them, what's the point? I mean, it's just like being another person altogether.'

'I think some people do,' answered her husband. 'Bigelow is quite clear about it. The terrible food, having to be brave, stuff like that. Dreams about it, too, he said. In some kind of contact with the Other Side. He's a plain, card-carrying lunatic. You'd never know it to look at him.'

'Well, Alfie,' said his mother, 'perhaps we should hypnotise your father and find out about *his* earlier lives. What do you reckon, a cave man maybe ...?'

They were walking home from school together, Alfred slightly behind Josephine. He was looking carefully at the pavement.

'I say, Allie, this is just like old times. Do you remember – when you used to go to school *every day*, like the rest of us?'

'It's all a bit hazy, now, Mabe. So much has happened to me since those carefree, childhood days.'

'It must have been terrible in the trenches. The flies. The heat. You still look worn out. What is it?'

'I'm just knackered because of school. I'm out of practice.'

'Perhaps you'd like to take a breather? There's a seat outside the library for people like you, before you go up the hill. War veterans, that sort of thing ...'

They walked on together. Josephine stopped.

'Look, what *is* it Allie?'

Alfred said nothing. He felt desperate and disembodied. Daily life at home or at school had no element of reality for him. It seemed an eternity since he used to go about normal things without nagging anxiety at the back of his mind, and every morning he was more exhausted than when he had gone to bed the night before. He couldn't concentrate properly during lessons. When he tried to fix on what the teacher was saying the words stood one by one on their own, not in sentences, and there was no graspable meaning. When he stopped listening altogether his mind raced away like a kite off its string, soaring somewhere across the horizon.

He was not even really listening now to Josephine, who was literally pulling on his arm. He was anticipating being upstairs later, in the house, after supper.

Was he safe …?

Would they come …?

'Well, I think you're *stupid*. You always tell me things. You always have done. It's stupid to be so secretive, like you've got some terrible *disease* and won't tell anybody. What if it's infectious?'

'I haven't got an infectious disease, Jose. I just feel a bit low, that's all.'

'What is this then, adolescence? I'm *fed up* about it, Allie. I'd tell you if I caught the Black *Death*, or something.'

'I think I'm coming down with scurvy.'

'Dandruff, you mean?'

'Listen, Mabe, I'm OK. When I get to the point of having to make my will, you'll be the first to know. I'd like you to have my CD collection, I can tell you now.'

'Fine. That's all I wanted to hear. What about the roller skates? Or, you could hand those over for my birthday tomorrow …'

'You'll have to wait for them. I have your present already.'

Chapter Twenty-Seven

'You know, Mum, I'm really *worried* about Alfred,' said Josephine to her mother, who was washing up after Sunday lunch. She stood holding a plate in one hand and a tea towel in the other.

'You are, dear?'

'He's behaving quite oddly.'

'But he's fully recovered from that horrible thing now, isn't he? At least, Mrs Appletree said she thought he was quite back to normal. He seemed perfectly alright yesterday at teatime.'

'Yes, it's not that he's still *ill* or anything. He just seems *different*.'

'Ah, different. Perhaps he's in love. Are you sure it's not just a case of boys will be boys and all that?'

'I've no idea what that really means.'

'Nor have I, now you mention it. Shall we ask your father? He was one once, so he claims.'

This and similar conversations did nothing to reassure Josephine, who was, truth to tell, justifiably anxious about Alfred. He was polite in conversation, but as if he were really thinking about something else altogether. And still a good bit thinner than before he was ill.

He had come for tea the day before for Josephine's fourteenth birthday. It was just a family thing with some old school friends and a couple of cousins down from Norfolk whom they'd met before, in front of whom she didn't mind blowing out a bundle of candles. For her actual birthday celebration she would be going to a show and a restaurant one evening with her *real* friends – and *no boys*, as she explained to Alfred – later in the week. Alfred had looked pale, didn't quite finish his cake, and had little to say. He didn't even stay very long. Even when he had offered Josephine her present he had been uncommunicative, just handing her the small parcel with a peculiar smile. She had opened it after everyone had gone home. It was jolly weird, she thought, carefully preserving the wrapping paper as her mother was always telling her. For some reason Alfred had given her a grubby and faded old book about rope-making and knots. Did he think she was a *girl guide* or something?

She went to the phone. She dialled half the number and then replaced the receiver. After a moment she dialled again.

'Alfie, it's Josephine.'

'Hi.'

'Fancy doing something … going somewhere?'

'Not now. I'm trying to finish my damn essay.'

'*Still?*'

'Come off it, Mabe, this is a serious work.'

'OK. OK. Fine. Lovely to talk to you. Thank you for my present. Just what I've always wanted. You really shouldn't have. Thank you for calling. Please don't …'

'You called me, actually.'

'… hesitate to call back if we can be of further assistance. We think you are a secretive *pig*. Please leave a message after the beep.'

'I'll phone you, Jose. I've just got to …'

'Yes?'

'Write a few thousand words. Lay a few ghosts. Nothing serious.'

Chapter Twenty-Eight

It came to Alfred that weekend that the shipboard dreams themselves had probably stopped, now that they were being replaced by a different and more sinister danger. He sensed that from now on he was going to be vulnerable whenever he was alone in the evening. When he was tired, and especially when he had to write about the pirates themselves, he might have to expect another visitation.

For two days he experimented. If he blotted them out firmly, and especially if he did other homework, the evening would be quite normal – nothing strange would happen. On the Thursday night he tried doing his pirate writing while watching television, sunk in the middle of the huge sofa in the sitting room, his books around him between the pillows. He was finding a way to portray the pirates as believable individuals.

Captains were often brutal men, wrote Alfred, with some difficulty. There was no hard surface on the sofa to support his papers. *Their job was to exercise control over a mixed crowd of ruffians, free-booters and killers. Often the only way they could do this was by deliberate displays of cruelty, although some, we can be sure, just enjoyed inflicting pain or misery for its own sake …*

His parents were surprised to find him downstairs since Alfred was not normally much of a television-watcher. It made no difference, however. One way or another, he thought, the pirates would be ready for him. It grew cold in the sitting room and eventually he plodded upstairs and fell into bed.

All was quiet.

Alfred woke sharply and suddenly in the darkness. Something had disturbed him, but as he lay, half out of the blankets, he couldn't tell what. He froze, taut as he listened for the slightest sound. He tried to breathe steadily as if he were deeply asleep. All was quiet, and he was beginning to think there was nothing there, but he went cold all over when he heard a low whispered voice:

'He's over there, Captain. In his … bunk. Strange sort of bunk, isn't it?'

'Yes. Funny sort of place altogether. No wonder we have such trouble with him.'

'We taking him now?'

'No. Could be tricky, if he gets noisy. What we'll do is come back with two of the others.'

'Should we gag him first?'

'That, or my pistol …'

'So when do we come?'

'Whenever. Now we've seen how the land lies. We've got other things to do first. He'll not be going anywhere, after all, will he, while he's busy *writing*?'

They laughed, their voices fading away gradually. Alfred lay rigid for an eternity. He got out of bed and found his earphones. He tuned the radio to a bland, comforting station and eventually fell asleep to the mindless chatter of a late-night phone-in programme.

Chapter Twenty-Nine

Alfred couldn't eat supper on Friday evening; he just sat there with an untouched plate. His mother sighed to herself but said nothing, following a warning look from her husband. He had a strong feeling that Alfred 'needed some space'.

The constant threat of the pirates' reappearance in the house hung over Alfred and clogged his very limbs. He stared round the dining room as if he'd never seen the wallpaper or pictures before. He felt trapped and powerless and on his own. He looked at his parents in turn, wondering what they would say if he asked them for help. He couldn't. He just *couldn't*.

While they were drinking their coffee he excused himself and went slowly into the hall. He picked up the telephone and looked at the scrap of paper with the number he had been carrying around for some time. He dialled. The phone was answered almost immediately so that he had no time to prepare his words.

'Hello, Fiona Cholmondley speaking … Hello?'

'Er, hello. Is Dr Hugo there please?'

'No, I'm afraid not. Is that the boy from the newsagents?'

'Er, no. Will he be there soon?'

'He's in Philadelphia at the moment, I'm afraid. He'll be back on Tuesday evening. He's at a conference and he's got to give a lecture.'

'Oh.'

'Would you like me to give him a message?'

'It's all right. Or perhaps you could tell him Alfred called. About pirates.'

'About pirates. Fine. Anything else?'

'I'm in trouble.'

'With pirates? You funny boy. Well, I'll tell Hugo. He'll be able to help, I'm sure. Next week. Just hang on till then …'

Chapter Thirty

The next time, nearly a week later, their voices were louder. They were over by his desk, their heads together, talking intently. There were other noises: he heard a muffled curse from the passage outside and realised that they must have brought crew members with them too. He lay rigid with fear. After a few days of respite he had begun to think it might all have blown over, but they had come back again, and in force. What should he do? Perhaps he could …

'Hey, look at *this*, Captain,' said the first mate.

Alfred unscrewed one eye and saw the pirates examining his aquarium.

'Davy Jones locker itself. And a two-master on the bottom. Will you look at that? And I've never seen fish like those before. Fancy it in your cabin, maybe?'

'Maybe indeed, Deadeye. Tell Ropey to bring it when we take the boy.'

The captain was turning over things on his desk: his calculator, the PlayStation, other bits and pieces. The stegosaurus skeleton fell over with a clatter, not for the first time.

'Nothing else here worth taking. Load of rubbish. Let's do it.'

Alfred felt his very toes clinch with fear, and in fact he could hardly breathe for terror. But part of his mind was still asking: 'You are not afraid of them *there*; why be so petrified *here*?' 'Because,' he answered back from his tightened innards, 'if they take me from here I'll never be able to get back again.' Or perhaps he would be able to dream himself back when asleep on the ship? Or was he dreaming now? What would happen about school? Or exams?

'So, we take him now?'

'We do. This is the right time. I don't want to have to come back here again. If this doesn't work we'll look elsewhere. He's not worth the trouble.'

'OK. I'll get Stumps.'

Alfred remembered Stumps. He couldn't hold a cutlass properly after what the first mate referred to as his 'battle manicure'. But he was built as of oak, with no detectable neck and legs like mainmasts.

'What we do is wrap him in that sheet before he knows what is happening, and truss him like a crocodile. Then, you take one end, I'll take the other. And if he makes any noise – you know what to do.'

Alfred wondered about his chances of making a break for it. He could fling himself out of bed and dash down to his parents' room.

It was hopeless. There were the two rugby internationals leaning against the doorway; he'd never get through. And anyway, what could his father do against four armed pirates? He'd probably hide under the bedclothes, behind his mother. She might give them what for, though. Alfred felt a burst of hysterical laughter welling up inside him at the idea of his mother in her nightdress taking on a quartet of murderous buccaneers. More likely, she'd offer them tea in the kitchen, once she had put on her dressing gown. 'Are you all hungry?' she'd ask, opening the fridge …

He felt the captain's breath on his cheek and could smell the first mate.

'He'll need a telescope, by the way,' said the captain. 'The brat lost the other one in the sea.'

There was an alarming crash from behind them.

Ropey was struggling with the aquarium, but it slipped from his embrace and landed on the desk. Was it broken? What about his fish?

'Alfie?' he heard his mother call from below. '*Alfie*, what has *happened*? Are you all right?'

He could hear someone coming up the stairs. He sat up in bed and swung his legs over the side, uncaring. He saw the welcome burly shape of his father against the light in the hall, and his thudding heart nearly burst.

'Look *out*! Look *out*!' called Alfred from the very depths of his being, but no sound came out of his mouth, and when he looked round the darkness of his room, the pirates had gone.

They sat in the kitchen, all in their dressing gowns. It was past three in the morning.

'What on earth were you doing, my mysterious wee boy? Sleepwalking?' asked his father.

Alfred was sitting quite close to him, swinging his legs on the stool.

'Maybe. It was the aquarium, it fell on the desk, somehow.'

'Had you moved it then? Funny thing to happen. Still, it's all in one piece, and so are you. Certainly woke the fishes up.'

'Never mind, Frederick. Alfie's fine. That's all that's important. You did give me a start. Are you all hungry?' She opened the fridge ….

After the later-than-midnight feast no-one felt like going back to bed. Alfred's father went upstairs with him to have another look at the aquarium. Alfred was not surprised to discover that all his fish were dead. The big angel fish and his two lieutenants were lying in the murk on the bottom. He wondered whether it was the bump that was responsible or whether they had just died of fright when the mate looked them in the eye.

'They've lasted pretty well,' said Mr Appletree, uncertain how to interpret his son's expression, 'but perhaps I ought to have insured them …? Just a joke. I tell you what, why don't you and I go down to the pet shop on Friday after school and invest in some replacement models? A couple of lively young piranhas, for example. What do you say?'

He yawned. So did Alfred.

116

Chapter Thirty-One

It was odd being collected from school, but Alfred felt excited as if he were much younger as his father parked the car. You could never tell whether the pet shop was actually open or not. Half the windows were boarded up, the others plastered with posters and notices with special offers. It was hard to breathe inside too, with all the mixed-up smells competing on top of the sawdust. There was a dank wall of fish tanks and Mr Appletree was soon in conversation with the assistant about which species were guaranteed not to eat which. Alfred looked around the patient menagerie. It was a bit like a small-scale Ark, he thought, all the animals ready to be liberated and out in the air again.

There was a squawk behind him and his head whizzed round. There in the corner, in a luxurious old brass cage, was a parrot. An honest-to-goodness, full-sized, green jungle-type macaw. Alfred gazed at it with his mouth open. It had just never occurred to him that it might be possible to *buy* a parrot and take it *home*. He was awestruck by the possibilities.

'*Dad* – ' he called, 'look at this. Can we … *could* we … ?'

His father wandered over holding a transparent bag with several fish cruising round inside, followed attentively by the shop assistant. The parrot looked down at the three of them.

'Does he talk?' asked Alfred.

'Everybody asks me that,' replied the man. 'They always do the *Pretty Polly* routine and never get a squeak out of him. Can't say I blame him. But he's a wily old bird. Depth of personality. I always say he only talks when no-one is listening.'

'Sounds like me,' said Mr Appletree.

'Can we buy him, Dad?' pleaded Alfred after a pause.

'Five hundred and twenty quid,' said the man, firmly. 'Cash. With cage. An antique, that cage. And three months seed thrown in.'

Mr Appletree made a wide dismissive gesture.

'I think for today we will settle for piscine species,' he said. 'It's a lot of money … your mother … they are a lot of *work*, too, aren't they, parrots?' he concluded, turning to the man.

'Not really,' said the man. 'This one knows the ropes. Been in films. Clean up the cage once in a while. Teach him Chinese or juggling if you like. Never regret it.'

'What is he called?' asked Alfred. He looked the parrot straight in the eye. He wasn't sure, but he thought that the parrot winked at him.

'I call him Captain,' said the man, 'but he had a terrible name when he came in. What was it now? … Oh yes, Methuselah.'

'Alfred, you're wanted on the phone … Alfred … ALFRED!'

Alfred jumped. He was lying on the floor again, staring at the light bulb above his head in a completely different daydream. He had been in a jungle, trying to learn Methuselah's language. He picked up the phone in the upstairs hall and heard his mother replace her receiver.

'Is that Alfred?'

'Yes.'

'Oh, good. This is Dr Cholmondley speaking. I've got back from America. I gather that you called about a problem with pirates?'

'Er, yes.'

'Is it still a problem?'

'Yes. It's got worse.'

'Anything I could help with? … Hello … Hello …? Oh … I see. Do I take it that this is not a thing to be talked about over the phone?'

'Yes, exactly,' replied Alfred.

'Well, look, why don't you come over on your bike tomorrow morning? We can have a chat. We're right opposite the pub, once you find our road. What's it called? *The Crown and Anchor*. It has a painted sign. Anyway, come round about eleven. I'll be up in the rigging, probably, when you get here.'

'*Rigging?*'

'In a manner of speaking. Oh, and bring an old hat when you come …'

That was good news. His heart lightened. Perhaps if he could start talking to the historian he would be able to get round to the really indigestible stuff that was making his life a nightmare. There was definitely no-one else. Maybe this was the answer. He felt infinitely better.

Chapter Thirty-Two

When it came to the next morning though, Alfred was really regretting that he had agreed to visit Dr Cholmondley. The phone call a few days before had been made in desperation, and now he was irritated with himself about the whole thing, but he couldn't think of a way of getting out of it.

It was a while since he had used his bicycle, and of course the back tyre was flat. He kicked the front one. That seemed a bit flabby too. Then he found that his bicycle pump was hiding somewhere. He never carried it on the bike in case it was stolen, but it wasn't in its proper place and the one on his mother's bike had lost the little tube that connected to the valve. Blast! He slouched grumpily into the utility room to get a bowl of water …

An hour later Alfred rang Dr Cholmondley's doorbell. There was quite a wait, and then he heard a loud bump, and a voice calling 'Hold on, don't go away!' The door opened and he saw Dr Cholmondley, wearing a mixture of colourfully speckled clothes and holding a paint roller.

'Come in, Alfred. I won't actually shake hands lest you turn white in the process. It is a pleasure to see you. You are just in time to witness my seldom-seen Michelangelo impression. Did you bring headgear or do you need a portion of old sheet?'

Alfred had forgotten about bringing a hat.

'Step this way. I shall find you a covering. I am busily transforming what I considered to be our perfectly comfortable home to a model

of magazine-style splendour. Our younger daughter Elizabeth is to be married next month and it is anticipated that coach-loads of relatives on both sides will descend like locusts on our normally peaceful establishment. The shabby paintwork and gloomy ceilings that have sheltered us so faithfully all this time will no longer do. This is where I come in. Those hypercritical great aunts have to be able to see their reflection in the paintwork by the time I am finished.'

Alfred grinned.

'What has happened with your new book?'

'Oh that just has to wait. Once the house is beaming like a lighthouse and my daughter is married off I might be able to sneak back unobserved to the sixteenth century. Anyway, come up and admire the Sistine chapels. I've done one and a half ceilings this morning, and we'd better finish the first coat before Mrs C. gets back for the inspection.'

They tramped up the stairs together to the landing, which was encumbered by wardrobes and upended beds. There was a home-made structure involving ladders and planks that enabled the artist to reach his ceiling.

'That is the rigging then?' asked Alfred, rather impressed.

'It is. It sways in a high wind, as all rigging should. Not that I need tell an old hand like you that, need I?' Dr Cholmondley climbed carefully into position.

'Not really,' answered Alfred absently. He didn't want to talk about pirates at all, but was more interested in having a go at painting the ceiling with a roller.

'The thing about this job is that your shoulder starts to ache diabolically and flicks of paint get into your hair and eyebrows. The more enthusiastic you are, the whiter your hair becomes. Do you think that might be true of life in general, young Alfred?'

Alfred, wanting to be helpful, stirred the huge tub of paint at the foot of one of the ladders with what appeared to be the lower end of an old tennis racket.

'Could be. Where does hair loss fit in?'

'That's a different type of overhead stress. You know, Alfred, you look a mite thinner than since I last saw you. Have you been overdoing the bookwork or is it just the weightlifting?'

'I'm still trying to write my essay.'

'Oh, that. When's it got to be in?'

'Next Friday.'

'Or you'll have to walk the plank in front of the whole class?'

'Yep.'

'So, what's been holding you up? You were going great guns when I last saw you.'

'Well, it's hard to say.'

'You needn't worry. Many writers have difficulty getting started.'

'That's not really my problem. It's more the carrying on. I can't find a way to describe it.'

'But you're a bit of a pirate expert by now, aren't you?'

'Mm.'

Dr Cholmondley paused in his work and smoothed over a ripple in the painted surface.

'What's the problem, then?'

'I can't write about them. They're too … close now. The more I try to write, the more they intrude.'

'How do you mean, *intrude*?'

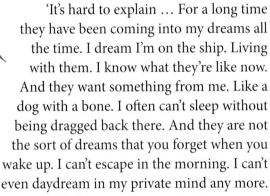

'It's hard to explain … For a long time they have been coming into my dreams all the time. I dream I'm on the ship. Living with them. I know what they're like now. And they want something from me. Like a dog with a bone. I often can't sleep without being dragged back there. And they are not the sort of dreams that you forget when you wake up. I can't escape in the morning. I can't even daydream in my private mind any more.

And whenever I try and write my essay something tugs at me. They … laugh at me. I … hear it, in my room. They've … come there to … get me. I think they'll be back for me, too. They can't leave me alone, somehow …'

Dr Cholmondley looked down from his ladder.

'Was it like this when you came to the library?'

'It had begun. Just the beginning. But I didn't know then what it was going to be like.'

'Have you thought of writing about something completely different for your essay?'

'I can't now. I have to finish this. I need to deal with them.'

'Tell me, Alfred, do you think they'll go away when you've finished the essay?'

'I don't know. Maybe. Actually, no, I'm not sure they will.'

'Can you see the ship now, while we're talking together here?'

'No. But if I let myself stop listening to you and just stared into space, I would be able to smell the salt and hear the wind in the sails, like an appetiser. If I tasted them properly I'd be right back, right in the thick of it.'

'Have you told anyone else about them?'

'Nobody at all. They would think I'm completely mad, wouldn't they?'

'Why do you feel you can talk to *me* about it?'

'I don't know. You're a real historian. I suppose I thought that you could prove to me that they're all dead. And not alive somewhere, waiting.'

That wasn't all. It had occurred to Alfred that perhaps something similar to what was now happening to him had once happened to Dr Cholmondley, but he couldn't quite bring himself to frame the question.

'Hmm. You know, Alfred, the world is a much more mysterious place than most people are prepared to acknowledge. I don't think you're mad at all, and nothing in what you say seems strange to me. Of course, one could say different things in reaction to it.'

'What do you mean?'

'Well, if I were a psychiatrist I should probably conclude that you were a sensitive and impressionable young man with a vivid imagination, and that you had been devoting far too much time to reading and thinking about pirates. I would suggest that you had become obsessed with the subject, and that this was beginning to create in you a certain paranoia with consequent accompanying delusions.'

He paused. Alfred said nothing. The roller moved steadily across the ceiling.

'After a dozen or so sessions in my consulting room I should recommend that you take up vigorous outdoor sports with members of your peer group, forgetting all about pirates, and send your father a whopping bill.'

Alfred laughed.

'However, I am not a psychiatrist.'

Dr Cholmondley put down his roller.

'On the other hand, if I were an unsympathetic schoolmaster I might say that you were a lazy scheming scamp who couldn't be bothered to sit down for once and write a long-overdue essay, and that you needed a dose of serious discipline in the ranks of the navy to knock the nonsense out of you.'

Alfred said nothing.

'However, being a muddle-headed and aging historian who has read far more nonsense than is good for anybody, and spent far too long trying to resurrect characters who are long and safely dead, I should say that your position raises some very interesting questions. Who knows, for example, but that you were once a pirate boy yourself, two or three hundred years ago, and that by some funny crossover of the wires you can be here and there at the same time? That would explain everything rather neatly, wouldn't it? I'm not saying that this *is* the explanation, but there are people who would suggest it quite matter of factly. Not reincarnation, but more of a system of parallel worlds. Perhaps you found a crack between them? Or, maybe our psychiatrist is nearly on the right track. Maybe you want to write such a brilliant essay that your imagination has gone into overdrive in the attempt to reconstruct the most convincing and plausible picture of pirates as they really were, and keeps worrying away at the problem while you are trying to sleep, or eat your breakfast cereal, and you have brought them to life in the process.'

'Whatever the explanation,' he continued, 'there is the separate problem that something in the end will have to be done about it. We can't have you getting thinner and thinner perpetually, for one thing. Where would that end? And there are other things in life than school essays and pirates.'

He looked carefully at Alfred.

'I think it will sort itself out. I think that now you'll be able to write this essay. You've got whole days ahead of you, all the time in the world. I'm going to give you one of my own special American pencils to take with you. They're not round, but triangular, and fit perfectly between your fingers without sliding about while you're thinking. I always use them for writing articles. I guarantee it will make all the difference. Perhaps the minute you have written those magic words *The End* at the bottom of the final page it will stop. The dreams and the visits. Perhaps not. Maybe something else or someone else will intervene, in a way that you might not expect, to break the link and leave you to yourself again. Let me just look into this handy crystal ball a moment … Yes, I see a great historian's essay and a fatter, smiling Alfred …'

The front door banged below and a female voice called 'Hu-go! We're ba-ack!'

Dr Cholmondley sighed arduously and winked at Alfred.

'Alfred, something tells me they've returned. There could be coffee and cake in it for us, if we're lucky. This coat has to dry anyway. What say we knock off for half an hour and go and join the ladies …?'

Chapter Thirty-Three

A watcher well acquainted with Alfred Appletree might have noticed a new lightness in his step as he made his way to school some days later. The famous essay was safe in its folder, deep in the centre portion of his school rucksack. No-one was going to steal it, and it was not going to burst into spontaneous combustion. Even earthquakes, he thought, would have to wait until he had passed safely by.

It was a good feeling to be rid of the millstone. He walked along, kicking a pebble. There was a freshness in the air to which anyone would respond, and Alfred hummed to himself. It would be really good to hand the thing over, right into Willoughby's hands.

He turned finally into the long main road where the school was situated. There were groups of children ahead of him, and stragglers behind. Alfred swung his rucksack and whistled under his breath.

As he approached he noticed that the school entrance was, unusually, partly blocked by a monster yellow lorry. It was an oversize refuse truck, parked right by the gates, with a plastic doll jammed over the bonnet as a sort of trophy, but no driver to be seen behind the windscreen.

The lorry cast a deep shadow over the pavement, and he shivered as he drew alongside. Three men in overalls stood at the tail end, heads bent together, supervising the metallic jaws crushing the rubbish from the local bins. Two were quite stocky, one slender and powerful, and, for some reason … almost familiar. Alfred noticed their *earrings*. Earrings always looked funny on grown-ups, fathers pretending to be tough guys …

He drew close and as he did so one of the men in blue overalls turned to look directly at him. He was sunburned and lithe-looking, sporting a black headband like a Wimbledon star.

Alfred's blood stopped in his veins.

The man had only one eye. The other was covered by a patch on a tarry black string. The good eye looked steadily at Alfred and winked.

This was no *dustman*.

The pirate grinned at him. The other two turned as he stood, paralysed with horror, and nudged one another.

128

So here they were again. Flesh-and-blood pirates, come to get him. In disguise, this time, but outside his own school, in broad daylight. Giant-size bullies. He wasn't going to get away from them after all.

The older pirate murmured something to his mate and all three moved towards him.

'NO!' shouted Alfred and he rushed frantically into the road right between the moving cars, fortunate to reach the other side. Several drivers honked at him, or shouted. There were three boys from his year together on the opposite pavement, not friends of his, waiting to cross. He joined them without saying anything, staying right next to them, and found himself re-crossing the road down-wind of the lorry.

The three pirates stood there, watching relentlessly as he went through the gates. Alfred tried not to look at them. As he went by, though, he saw them nod to one another and there was a guffaw. He crossed the playground, feeling their eyes boring into his back. The rucksack bumped against his leg. His pirate essay, incriminating them, was safe inside.

They *wouldn't* come in the *school*.

They *couldn't*.

Or could they?

What should he do? Whom could he tell?

Chapter Thirty-Four

Mr Willoughby slowly put down Alfred's pirate manuscript. His wife had recently presented him with some new handkerchiefs and he shook one fully out to its maximum extent like a great white flag, and removed his glasses. They needed, at this stage, he thought, a good polish. He leaned back in his chair. His desk at home for the last few days had been covered with folders full of history projects. Some this year were really excellent, thorough and convincing, with super maps and drawings.

The Jellicoe girl, for example, had done a fine piece of work on the old and new local police stations, drawing an imaginative parallel between the old, small station (friendly coppers on the beat) and the brand-new flashy complex (electronic policemen in cars). She had hunted up the constable who was often near the crossing by the school in the old days (who would have thought he was still going strong?), and he had provided lots of local details about community relations. An excellent topic, A-minus or maybe even A, thought Mr Willoughby. The cover had a funny drawing of the old school crossing, with a police car, flashing light hard at work, reluctantly slowing down to allow an elderly policeman wheeling a pushbike to cross in safety. *Some fine feeling for history here and first-rate illustrations* he had written on the last page.

But then this thing of young Appletree's – it was ambitious for his age group, unusually so, tackling a very large and complex area (the relation between truth and fiction, history and romance), and head-butting some even bigger ones (how do we know what we think we know, and how do we even know it's true anyway?). The trouble was that Alfred, in taking on the question of pirates, had gone round in circles. He had tried (like a good historian) to find out the truth about them – even hunting out books at the university library (and how many kids had he known to do that, he asked himself) – but …

What was that opening paragraph again?

Most people have grown up with pirates, taking them for granted, believing them to belong somewhere with Robin Hood and people like that, not knowing how dangerous they really were. But they really were. Like bullies that pick on people in the street, they preyed on innocent sailors and traders using terror to intimidate them into non-resisting. Violence with them became a habit, and one that corrupted them, so that even moral ones became immoral.

Some descriptions were extraordinarily vivid, shocking even, and somehow totally convincing. It's almost, thought Mr Willoughby, as if he'd dug up an old pirate himself and tackled him with a tape-recorder.

And the handwriting! It lurched madly between clarity and scribbling.

And there were no illustrations except the one small, rather eloquent ink sketch on the cover. It showed a traditional pirate's treasure chest, its gnarled wooden sides bound with bands of iron, much scarred and battered. There was a padlock lying beside it and the lid was open.

'Yo-ho-ho and a bottle of rum' thought Mr Willoughby, swinging his glasses carelessly to and fro.

The chest itself was, however, quite empty.

'So, what mark do I give him?' he wondered. *A-plus* for the idea and the effort, certainly; *D* for historical method; anything between *A* and *D* for presentation. What to do? The fact was, he thought, young Appletree had expended a great deal of historically oriented *effort*. That was clear from every page. *B*? *B-minus*? *C-plus-plus*? Or maybe *A-minus*? 'Yes, I think, all in all, *A-minus* would be right ...'

Chapter Thirty-Five

They were lying in long grass at the back of the park. Half-term break was nearly over. It was surprisingly warm. Josephine propped her chin on one hand and looked down at Alfred.

'Allie, you've *got* to tell me what's been going on with you. You've got to. I can help you. Maybe I'm not the only person who can, but I know I can. Like when you pulled me out of the deep end when I would have drowned that time.'

'Mabe, if I tell you what the problem really is you'll laugh. Or think I'm completely screwy.'

'Try me, Alfie. I won't, really.'

'It's … those pirates. You know I did do them for my topic in the end. It's the pirates from all those years ago. I started writing about them now, and dreaming about them at the same time. They seem to be alive somewhere, continuing their existence. They've been in my room. They're here. I think they resent my writing about them and want to take me back where they can control me.'

'What on *earth* do you mean, Alfie?'

'I dream I'm on their ship. Right in the middle of it all. Different places, or things happening, but the same ship. And I only ever meet a few of the crew. And now, if I try not to go to sleep, they come to my room. I can hear them talking and I can almost see them. Actually, I have seen them. Even outdoors. Near the school.'

'The *school*? What do they *want* from you?'

'They believe I'm part of their world, I think, but I don't understand why it's important to them. I irritate them or interest them. I don't know which. It's not every time I go to sleep, not even every week. But when I do dream about them it's more real than life. Sometimes it's as if they wait for me to come back so they can carry on. Like a stopped video. I thought at first nothing happened when I wasn't there, but now I know it does. I'm not always in the same place, and sometimes terrible things happen without me. I think they're my fault.'

'And they all take it for granted when you do come back?'

'Yes, Jose, exactly; that's exactly it. They're like a film that's being shown inside a cinema while you're outside. The film keeps running. And if you do go in, you see the film, and when you come out, you don't, but the film continues anyway without you. And the time's all different. Completely different. I never know how much has gone by when I get back.'

'But what do they want from *you*, Alfie? You're supposed to be a schoolboy at school. What can they possibly want?'

'Who knows, Jose? I don't …'

They fell silent, each thinking of the strangeness of it all. Alfred lay back beside Josephine, staring up at the sky, and then he fell asleep, his head hard against her arm. She felt his breathing slow down, and although her own arm was at an awkward angle she fell asleep too …

Chapter Thirty-Six

This time they were on the ship together. They were out on deck in the half-light, thankfully alone, standing close beside one another in the wind. The ship was being buffeted more violently than Alfred had ever known it. Spray was rushing up over the side and the deck was beginning to roll alarmingly.

Alfred looked at Josephine. She said nothing, but stared back at him with wide eyes. He could see that she was just beginning to understand. *Would she get seasick?* She always made a beeline for the worst kind of nausea-inducing rides when they went to fairgrounds. Perhaps she would be alright.

It was dead peculiar that there was no-one about. Probably they were eating below. It was quickly growing dark and there were only one or two lights on deck. They both held tightly onto the rail. *What could she be thinking?* The ship moved beneath them, her compact shape settling into the uneven sea, determined despite the storm. Someone must be at the wheel behind them, probably roped in place for security, and someone else would surely appear before long. He thought again of Louis, on duty above, left to his own company in all possible weathers. He peered upwards, but it was impossible to make out if there was another small figure in position.

Maybe that was why they wanted *him*?

But surely not. Not worth all the effort.

What on earth could he say to Josephine? She must be thinking that this was a dream, the sort that could be dispelled by pinching your arm. Should he tell her about Louis? It seemed appropriate now – he could visualise him so easily – but he still felt inhibited. It was too noisy, for one thing, to hold that sort of conversation. The wind, the water and the ship herself combined in such a volume of sound that it would be one of those hopeless shouted conversations with lots of 'What's?' Josephine was mouthing something now but he couldn't hear. Her hair was blowing all over her face, but her eyes were excited. *Thank God we didn't arrive in the middle of a battle*, he thought. Or any other bit of normal pirate business. She would never recover from the shock. He grinned at her. It really was peculiar that there was no-one on deck with them, but he was grateful for the fact. How would he introduce her? How could he explain that she was there?

He heard voices somewhere behind him. He motioned to Josephine quickly to follow him and they ran for cover, moving towards the back of the ship on the starboard side as the unseen crew member came up on the port. There were lights now on the poop deck and they could hear raised voices above and below. Perhaps it's a trick, thought Alfred. They are playing with us and will pounce.

They stood immobile in the shadows. Two of the pirates were there in front of them, talking together, sniffing the salt. He could feel Josephine staring open-mouthed at his former shipmates. He felt uncomfortable, and in a way even responsible for them, as when schoolmates who weren't real friends encountered his parents – the feeling of not knowing quite what they would do that might be embarrassing. But why should he care? The two gentlemen of fortune had clearly just eaten their fill below decks. One was picking his teeth with a knife, the other belched several times and bit off some tobacco. They looked convincing enough, mused Alfred, with all the right characteristics and accoutrements. Both were scarred and unwashed and ready for anything.

Josephine did not appear to be frightened at all, though. Perhaps she felt as if she were in the zoo, where you could get quite close to the most dangerous animals but they couldn't do you any harm. But there was neither fencing nor glass here, and Alfred knew what those pirates were capable of, if ordered, or just in the mood. Then the bald and not-so-youthful Jed – and what was the other called? Oh yes, Vincent – began to urinate over the side, downwind of his colleague. Fortunately his back was turned to them, but he felt Josephine begin to laugh. The pirates moved off. He turned to speak to her when he heard a door crash open behind them and the captain's roar echo about the ship:

'Where's that damnable scribe? Someone bring him here immediately or I'll have every man aboard flogged.'

Maybe *that* was it. Maybe the captain wanted to learn to read and write for himself and needed Alfred to teach him. *Could that be the explanation …?*

Then they were right in the captain's cabin together. The captain was beside himself, stamping about and shouting. The great book

ruled into columns lay open on the table. Two men were standing in the corner; one bleeding, the other sullen. A knife also lay on the table and a nearly empty bottle of rum.

'They've always squabbled over their gold, but it's worse than ever since you interfered. Now they don't believe your damn *book*, and they're always fighting about what the *writing* says. They've been playing dice for three days and there's another argument over the totals, and they want me to deal with it. I want discipline from these animals. You, pest, *work it out*! Or I'll throw you and your cursed book into jaws of blood.'

Josephine could feel Alfred trembling.

'But how can I possibly work out the figures if they have been playing when I wasn't watching?'

'Don't you answer me back, you unutterable wretch. I'll have you flogged to ribbons, and keel-hauled and fed to the sharks. You can't even imagine what I'll do to you. *You* had the bright idea of numbers, *you're* the clever-clever-writer: *sort it out*. I run a tight ship here dedicated to plunder, murder and other good times, and I won't have the hands wasting my time and theirs squabbling over your damned book-keeping when we should be enjoying the fruits of one bout of piracy or planning for the next.'

'You don't understand,' said Alfred. 'If the totals have been constantly ...'

'That *does* it,' said the captain, 'you're for the ocean floor in shredded, painful fragments.'

He opened the door again and bellowed for the first mate, who came running in immediately, a drawn cutlass in his hand.

'Take him and give him *number two* treatment, slowly,' said the captain. 'He's an utter nuisance. Make it last as long as possible. And her too, while you're about it. Females are not allowed on pirate ships anyway.'

Alfred turned white and staggered against the table. The other two pirates grinned at one another and the first mate moved towards him.

This was it, then. They were both going to die.

Could he reach the knife on the table?

Josephine stepped forward between Alfred and the captain.

'Why are you making such a fuss about *him*?' she said in her clear voice.

The pirates froze. The captain looked at her incredulously.

'He's no use to you. He's *useless* at maths. And he's never here, anyway, when he's needed.'

The captain nodded, despite himself.

'He's caused me nothing but trouble. Us running all over the cursed place. And all the captains want a bullion book now. It's catching on.'

'Get *another* boy,' said Josephine, 'a *reliable* one.'

She reached into her shoulder-bag and took out her purse. It was brightly coloured, decorated with 3-D stickers of pop stars and flashy emblems. She opened the purse carefully, shielding it with her left hand from their intrusive eyes. She took out a newish 5p piece.

'Here,' she said, 'a shilling. A *Queen's shilling*.'

She turned it over defiantly.

'And here's the Queen's head. I'm buying him back. Out of service. He's free to come with me. You agree?'

They looked sceptically at the modest coin.

'*All* the money,' said the captain flatly.

'What?'

'*All* the money.'

'And that money-bag,' added the mate.

140

'I'll need my bus pass and things,' said Josephine.

'The money and the bag and he's yours,' said the captain, after a pause. 'I'll get another. He's not the only number-writer in the world by any manner of means ...'

Chapter Thirty-Seven

They collected their bikes, which had fallen over together in a heap but not been interfered with, and made their way in silence out of the park. They cycled off towards home, Josephine in the lead, Alfred following, yawning at intervals, his front wheel wobbling slightly.

'Fancy an ice cream or something?' Josephine called over her shoulder.

'Yeah, Honey-bunch, a real cool idea,' drawled Alfred.

She turned round to look at him. Even ignoring the pathetic Hollywood imitation, Alfred's voice was different.

They parked outside the newsagents and went in. Alfred leaned dangerously into the ice box and spotted two of their favourite multicoloured rocket-shaped lollies buried in the ice at the back.

He pivoted on the edge and handed one back without looking, but Josephine didn't take it from him like a relay runner as he expected. She was digging irritably around inside her shoulder-bag and muttering to herself. In the end she turned the whole thing upside-down and tipped all the contents on the floor in front of the counter.

'Damn!' she said. 'Utterly *damn and blast!*'

The newsagent looked up in disapproval from her crossword.

'What is it, Jelly-babe? What on earth's the matter?' asked Alfred, nearly upside-down himself and trying to swivel round in a hurry on the edge of the freezer.

'*Disaster*. The ices are on you, Alfie. I can't believe I've *done* it. I seem to have lost my purse somewhere. How *stupid* can you get? But that's weird … here's my *travel card* and stuff … Oh well, never mind, I've been meaning to get a new purse for ages, and now I come to think of it there was hardly any money in it anyway …'

Alfred smiled quietly to himself, but said nothing. He was completely unafraid. He felt strong. He felt hungry. She had rescued him but he knew that nothing of his now-distant tormentors remained in her memory. He looked at the Jellicoe, picking up her possessions, and a brilliant idea came to him. He was going to save up for that great green parrot, Methuselah, in his antique cage and take him home to his house.

- The End -